The Cunning Man

Also by Celia Rees:

Point Horror Unleashed: *Blood Sinister*
The Vanished

The Cunning Man
·
Celia Rees

**SCHOLASTIC
PRESS**

Scholastic Children's Books,
Commonwealth House, 1-19 New Oxford Street,
London WC1A 1NU, UK
a division of Scholastic Ltd
London ~ New York ~ Toronto ~ Sydney ~ Auckland
Mexico City ~ New Delhi ~ Hong Kong

First published in the UK by Scholastic Ltd, 2000

Copyright © Celia Rees, 2000

ISBN 0439 01186 8

Typeset by M Rules
Printed by Cox and Wyman Ltd, Reading, Berks.

10 9 8 7 6 5 4 3 2 1

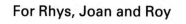
For Rhys, Joan and Roy

Chapter One

It was not always the same dream, but it always began in the same way. . .

They are going down to the beach, Finn, her brothers, Conn and Aidan, and Mum and Dad. A happy family outing. In the days when there *were* happy family outings. The weather is perfect. The sun is shining and the beach is crowded: children shouting, jumping in and out of the waves, laughing and calling as they play. Everything is fine – to start with. It is an ideal day.

But even at this point, Finn isn't sure. There is something about this beach that makes her uneasy. Backed by tall crumbling cliffs, it pitches steeply. The firm sand is deeply fissured, split with channels which run between towering rocks all piled up like giants' play bricks. The beach is not human scale at all. It is too deep, too big, the people are too small.

The uneasy feeling grows steadily, seeping in slowly at first, then welling up inside her, until she wants to shout out to all around her, to warn them that something terrible is going to happen. But she says nothing. In the dream she says nothing. She just carries on walking, following her family in their search for a likely spot to settle.

They go up and down the hollows and hummocks in the hard wet sand, burdened with bags and deck-chairs, picnic basket and beach toys. She cannot see the sea, only hear it, a dull far-off boom. Suddenly, for no reason, she feels slightly sick. She tastes sea water, thick in her throat like a premonition. The booming ceases. Replaced by the clack-clacking of pebbles, as the water withdraws.

This sound goes on for a long time. Too long. People look up, look around, as if alerted by some deep sense that something is wrong. Then they see it. Some are gesturing in frantic warning. Some are pointing. Happy beach cries turning to panicking screams as the enormous wave mounts and mounts. Some people race forward, still intent on play, jumping right in as the surf thunders down. For them there will be no coming back. They will be tumbled over and over, dragged backwards and forwards over the rocks and boulders, torn to pieces by the force of the water, because this is no ordinary sea. This is tsunami. Tidal wave.

Sand and shingle sucked up from the shore show inside the greeny glass wall, muddying the boiling foam as the waves thunder and fall. And always the sound: the huge explosive boom, like pressure waves inside the head; the slow, ominous drag back and back; the muffled clash as boulders the size of family cars roll and crash.

Everyone is running now, fleeing for their lives, belongings forgotten, children crying, babies wailing in the screaming scramble to get away from this murderous sea. But however fast they run, the sea is faster: faster than any human, faster than a horse can gallop, faster than a train. And each time the crash is followed by the dragging back, the little dream of escape before the nightmare wave.

Finn is running, too; going as fast as she can. Sometimes her legs are short, like when she was small, sometimes they are long and lithe, like they are now, but long or short, there is no escape. She looks from side to side, searching for Mum and Dad, Conn and Aidie; but there is no one she recognizes to left or right. She will die with strangers. In front of her is the sheer cliff face, behind her the sea.

She feels but does not see the last wave, looming above her head, tall as a tower block. She throws her head back to scream, but her final cry is lost in the crashing surf. Sea water pours into her mouth, rushing down her throat, making her gag and choke. Then there is nothing. She is being tumbled over and over inside the glass wall of water, bright hair floating, tangled in the dark weed.

The tide comes back, foaming pink, blood-stained and streaked, and all down its length the beach is empty. . .

The dream always ends in the same way. Finn lies unable to move, caught in a state between waking and sleeping, as if some paralyzing drug is working in her. Her mind is alive, her eyes are open, but her body is gripped by corpse-like stillness, her limbs frozen and useless, her mouth stretched open in a silent scream.

Chapter Two

In the morning, Finn knew she'd had the dream again. She woke with the thick salty taste still in her mouth and felt drained, with the remnants of a headache, like after a migraine. She hadn't had the dream in years, not since Dad left. Just like then, the dream was accompanied by something else, a kind of precognition. A sickening see-sawing sense that something bad was about to happen.

She lay for a while, listening to a sound familiar, yet unfamiliar: the tide on the shoreline. This was not the deep muffled boom and crash that made her sick to even think about; this was gentle, the soothing whisper of surf on sand. She relaxed a little. The sound must have penetrated her sleep, bringing the dream with it.

Finn got out of bed and went over to the window. They had arrived last night but it had been too dark to see much. There were no street lights here. The place they were staying in was called the Salt House. It stood on its own at the end of a long lane. There had been no moon. No stars. No comforting city glow. Finn had never known such blackness. It was like stepping into another dimension. Even the light of their torches had been rendered feeble. It was all they could do to find the front door.

It was different now. Last night's clouds had cleared away. It was still early, but the air was mild and already warming with the promise of a lovely day. She leaned out into it, her arms resting on the thick stone sill, taking in her new surroundings.

Down from the house was a little harbour. She could just see boat masts and a bit of the wall. To the right, a small promontory topped with pines shadowed the house. Out back was a rough patch of garden and beyond that the sea stretched away, mirroring the sky in a deep, almost Mediterranean blue. There was no wind. Waves broke white at a point far out, apart from that, the surface seemed almost motionless. The long curve of Westwater Bay stretched into the distance, waves creaming in to the wide flat beach in a thin curling hush of surf.

A loud ringing made her jump. Someone at the front door. The ringing stopped and then began again, more prolonged and insistent. Why didn't someone answer it? Where were the boys? Or Mum, for that matter. . .

"All right." Finn yelled down the stairs as the ringing started up again. "I'm coming, I'm coming!"

A blurred face loomed close through the ribbed glass panelling as she wrenched open the door.

"Hello," she said, holding the door half open.

"Hi." The young man stepped backwards. "I'm Mike. Mike Treherne." He grinned. The tanned skin round his light blue eyes creased and crinkled. "I've come about the work?" His eyebrows quirked up, they were bleached almost white. Streaky fair hair showed in a thick fringe under the bill of his baseball cap. "Can I speak to your Mum?"

Finn looked him up and down. He was tall, a little under six foot, she guessed, well-muscled and very brown. He wore a surfer T-shirt, ripped and faded. Baggy jeans, almost colourless, frayed by heavy wearing, rode low on his hips. He wore no socks and his unlaced work boots were old and cracked, scuffed white across the toe caps.

Finn turned away, suddenly aware that she was only wearing the T-shirt she slept in. He was scrutinizing her, too.

"Mu-um!" she yelled, "there's a—" she paused before saying "man". She judged him to be maybe seventeen, eighteen. Older than her, but not really a man yet, although his strong build and the fine golden stubble on his chin showed he was no longer a boy. She adjusted what she had been going to say. "There's a person to see you."

There was no reply from inside. They were left staring at each other.

"I'll go and see where she is," Finn said, pulling her T-shirt down at the front. "Hang on a minute."

She left him on the doorstep and went into the kitchen.

Her brothers were sitting at the table, mouths full of cereal.

"Where's Mum?" Finn demanded. "And why didn't either of you get the door?"

"We didn't know who it was," Aidan replied, slurping up another spoonful.

"So? You could still have answered. You're thirteen, not three. Who did you think it was, Frankenstein's monster?"

"Could have been." Aidan pretended to consider for a moment then shook his head. "Then we reckoned that was impossible. You being upstairs."

Aidan grinned up at her, brown eyes glinting. Conn spluttered, spraying milk and cornflakes all over the table. At three years younger, he was a miniature version of his brother. They looked just like each other, snorting with laughter, hair sticking straight up in identical copper-coloured convict cuts.

"Where's Mum?" Finn asked again.

"She's gone out for a walk."

"Did she take her sketch pad with her?"

"How should we know?" Conn dug into his cornflakes.

"Oh brilliant!" Finn rolled her eyes to the ceiling. "She could be out all morning. What am I supposed to do about this bloke?"

"What bloke?"

"The one standing on the doorstep. He's come about work, or something. Do either of you know anything about it?"

Conn shook his head.

"There's a note on the fridge." Aidan supplied. "Carole must have left it."

Auntie Carole was their mother's sister. They were here courtesy of her. It was her cottage.

Finn went over and pulled the paper out from underneath the fridge magnet.

"Expect a man about the work," she read. "Mr Treherne. *Mr* Treherne," Finn snorted. "He doesn't exactly look like a *Mr* to me. He doesn't look much older than you two and about as useful. . ."

Conn laughed, showing a mouth full of cornflakes and Aidan grinned.

"I wouldn't go on, if I were you," he said.

"Why not?" Finn demanded.

"He's not on the step anymore."

"Oh, hey." She whirled round to see Mike Treherne standing in the doorway. "I'm sorry. I didn't mean. . ." She left the sentence unfinished. She could feel herself going red.

"Mr Treherne's my uncle." The boy explained, his mouth twitching at her growing discomfort. "Sorry to disappoint you. Won't I do?"

"Yes, I'm sure. . ." Finn's blush deepened. "Perhaps one of you can go and look for Mum." Her brothers nodded, but made no move to go. "Right. OK, then. I'll go and put some clothes on. Be back in a minute."

Finn walked down the hall to the sound of male laughter. It was probably just Conn and Aidan, but she was sure she heard a deeper voice joining in. The blood thudded in her face as she mounted the stairs. She paused at the top, and leant her cheek against the cool banister, trying to hear if they were talking about her, wondering why she felt so humiliated.

She came downstairs, decently dressed in shirt and jeans, to find Mike Treherne quite at home. He was sitting at the kitchen table with a mug of coffee talking about football.

"Down on holiday?" he asked when she came in.

"Sort of." She flicked the kettle back on. "We're here for the summer. Looking after the place for my aunt. She owns it."

"I see." He stretched his long legs out and leaned back from the table, looking round at them. "Just you and your mum, is it?"

"Yes." Finn spooned coffee into a mug.

"Dad coming down later?"

Nobody answered. The boys, fizzing and bubbling a moment before, fell silent. Even Conn was subdued. Mike caught the look that passed between them. Their embarrassment spread to him.

"Oh, I'm sorry." He looked up at Finn. "Have I said the wrong thing?"

"Not really." Finn poured boiling water on to the granules. "He just doesn't live with us any more. That's all."

"That's why we're here," Aidan muttered. "Charity cases. We can't afford a proper holiday."

Finn gave him a warning look and the kitchen filled with awkward silence.

"My mother's not here at the moment." Finn poured

milk into her coffee. "I really have no idea when she'll be back. . ." she added without looking at him.

"Oh, right."

Mike Treherne got to his feet. He was being dismissed. Tourists. They were all the same. Especially English ones. Down here on holiday, thinking they owned the place. And they did, most of it, like the house he was standing in now.

"Thanks for the coffee. Tell your mother I called."

"Certainly," Finn replied, escorting him towards the door. "We can expect your *uncle*, when?"

"Whenever." He stared back at her, his blue eyes as cold as hers. That was a put down and he didn't care for it. "Someone'll be up this afternoon. I can see myself out."

Finn shrugged, whatever, and leaned on the unit, sipping her coffee. They had both reckoned without the boys.

"Hey! I thought you said you'd give us a game?" Conn was reaching for his football. "We could go down to the beach."

"Mum said we're not allowed," Aidan said quietly.

"That's to swim," Conn pointed out. "We're not supposed to go in the sea on our own. But we're not going for that. We're not exactly going to be playing underwater."

"No," Aidan brightened. "I suppose not."

"Anyway," Conn spun the ball up into the air and caught it. "Typical Mum. Fussing about nothing."

"She's not fussing about nothing," Finn frowned.

"Beaches can be dangerous. There won't be any life-guards down there. No one to help you if you get into trouble."

"But *he'll* be with us," Conn explained with the exaggerated patience he reserved for adults and older sisters. "And we're not going in the water, like I said. Come on, Finn. Don't be a pain."

"I'm sure *Mr* Treherne's got other things to do."

"Oh, please, call me *Mike*. I'd be delighted," he said to the boys, knowing that it would annoy her. He didn't know why she was being so antagonistic, but he could match like with like. "I was going down there anyway," he added with a smile. "Check on my boat."

"You've got a boat?" Conn's eyes grew wide with admiration. He'd got them now.

"It's only a little sailing dinghy. Don't get excited," Mike grinned down at the boy. "But, yeah, it's in the harbour."

"Will you take us out in it?" Conn asked, ignoring Finn's scowl.

Mike laughed. His laugh was deep and musical, like his voice.

"Someday. Maybe. Depends what your mum says. Meanwhile – do you want a game of football or not?"

He grabbed the ball off Conn and suddenly he was ten again. He held it high, throwing it from hand to hand, while the two smaller boys jumped around him like dogs.

"Not in the kitchen!" Finn shouted, but none of them took any notice. They threw the ball back and forth, laughing and yelling out of the back door and on down to the beach.

Boys were all the same, no matter what age, especially ones like him: big, sporty, outdoor types. Finn sat down at the table to drink her coffee, thinking that he was everything that she disliked. She preferred skinny, dark, waif-like creatures who looked like they only came out at night.

A sudden sound from outside made her jump. The mug jerked in her hand, spilling coffee. She looked up, startled. Her mother was out in the storm porch, smiling apology. The outer door had swung back much more violently than she'd intended, banging against the wall and bouncing back again.

"Hi, Mum. Where have you been?"

"Just up to the village to get a few things." Maggie Logan put the blue plastic shopping-bag on the kitchen table. "Sorry if I made you jump."

"I've just made some coffee. Fancy a cup?"

"Love one." Maggie sat down blowing strands of hair away from her face. "Phew! It's going to be hot."

Her pale face was faintly sheened and washed with pink. She shared her daughter's fair colouring, but her red hair was a shade darker than Finn's, her eyes a more definite green.

"What's the village like?"

"Not much there. Just a church and a few houses. A pub, of course, and a post office-cum-everything. It's pretty enough, but not chocolate box. I really liked it."

"Did you do any sketching?" Finn asked.

Her mum was an artist, but spent most of the year teaching at the local college which left her too drained to do any of her own work. One of the reasons they were down here was for her to try and recharge the batteries – get in touch with herself.

Maggie shook her head and took the camera from around her neck.

"Took a few snaps, but I've got loads of ideas. I really like it here. What do you think?"

Finn shrugged. It was too soon to judge. She had a suspicion there might be more to this trip than just a holiday visit. She'd heard Mum and Auntie Carole talking about this place. Auntie Carole had enthused; Mum had been envious. It was an emotion that she rarely felt. She had been quiet for days after, as if she was mulling something over. Then she'd phoned Carole, asking if they could stay for the summer.

"This *is* just a holiday," Finn hesitated and then went on. "You're not thinking of moving down here permanently?"

"I wouldn't do anything without discussing it with you and the boys, Finn. You know that." She looked around at the breakfast debris and then cocked her head to one side. "Where are they, anyway? The house seems awfully quiet."

"They're down at the beach."

"What?" Maggie Logan looked sharply at her daughter.

"It's OK, they aren't on their own. Don't stress. They're with someone."

"Who?"

"Someone called Mike Treherne."

"You've let them go off with a strange man?" Maggie's face registered further alarm. "I can't leave you for five minutes. He could be a child molester! Anything!"

"He's not all that strange," Finn replied. "And he's not a man. Not exactly. He's more a boy, about eighteen, I'd say. He came about some work Auntie Carole wants doing."

Her mother relaxed as she studied the note Finn handed to her. She wound a strand of hair round her fingers. She was wearing it tied back, because of the heat, but bits kept springing out.

"Carole did say something when she dropped the keys off," she said after a moment. "I remember now."

"You weren't here and I didn't know what to tell him. He went down to play football instead of waiting for you to come back."

"Well, I'm here now. You better call him up from the beach. First thing they can do is that door," she indicated the glass-roofed storm porch outside the kitchen. "It's practically off its hinges and the catch is as loose as anything."

Finn went down the little stony path that led to the bay. The sun shone down, strong already. She squinted into the bright white light, wishing that she had worn her sunglasses.

Things looked different down here from up at the

bedroom window. Smelt different, too. The little harbour reeked of rotten seaweed and ancient fish. The tide was right out, leaving the fishing boats and dinghies keeled over and stranded on fat banks of black ooze. Everywhere water sucked and gurgled. A river she had not even noticed carved through the mud and gushed down, spreading out across shoals of stones into a thin shining film rippling over the sand.

She looked beyond, to the beach proper, but didn't go on it. The saltwater seaweed stench brought her dream back to her, but that was not the reason for her hesitation. She was experiencing that feeling again: deja vu combined with premonition. Her stomach lurched. She felt light-headed and had to put out a hand to steady herself. She'd never seen this beach before this morning but something terrible had happened here, she just knew.

Chapter Three

By the afternoon, Finn had convinced herself that her fears were silly. The beach was just that, just a beach. She couldn't shun it. They were on holiday, after all.

She set off after lunch, carrying her beach towel, mat and a bag slung over her shoulder containing book, walkman and suntan lotion. A glance out to sea showed waves coming in low, barely rising to a foot or so, much to the disappointment of her brothers who were trying to body surf.

Her mother was keeping an eye on them while she sketched from the harbour wall. Finn waved on her way to find a patch of dry sand as far from the sea as possible. She unrolled her mat, spread her towel, and began applying high factor suntan lotion. Pale skin went with her red-gold hair and she never really tanned, just went a faint biscuit – if she was lucky. If she was *unlucky*, she'd burn and then peel – not an attractive prospect. She didn't want that to happen. It was the kind of thing that a boy like Mike Treherne would definitely find amusing. Just because it didn't happen to him. She didn't see why not. He had blond hair and blue eyes but, as her mother often pointed out to her, who said life was fair?

She thought about reading for a while, but then lay down, removing her sunglasses to avoid owl patches round the eyes. She had slept badly last night and soon her brothers' shouts and cries blended in with the calls of the circling gulls and gradually faded to nothingness.

She woke abruptly, aware of a shadow falling over her.

"Hey!"

Finn sat up quickly, her hot skin contracting as cold drops rained down. Her brothers capered round, howling with laughter, flicking water, their white skin pimpled, their hair black and spiked by the sea.

"Pack it in, will you?" She glared up at them, grabbing a towel to defend herself.

"Come on, Finn," Aidan grinned. "We've found something."

"Not interested." Finn moved to turn over. "Go away and leave me alone."

"Ah, come on." Conn's grin widened, to show the gap in his front teeth. "If you don't. . ."

"If I don't, what?" Finn squinted up, just in time to see the bucket Aidan was hauling back, ready to fling the contents. She moved as fast as she could, but was left gasping as the icy water cascaded down her back.

"Right!"

She was on her feet and after them. She was older and taller, her legs longer. She caught Conn easily, he was the youngest and at least a head shorter, but there was nothing to get hold of, he was as cold and slippery as an eel.

"Hey!" Conn squirmed out of the grip she had on his neck. "It was only a bit of fun! We do have something to show you!" He pleaded as she made another lunge for him. "We do!"

"OK, what is it?" Finn stood hands on thighs, panting from her dash down the beach. "And it better be good."

"It is." Aidan was beckoning, pointing to a pile of rocks stacked up like giant sugar cubes.

"No tricks?" Finn looked from one brother to the other.

They both shook their heads solemnly. "Absolutely no tricks."

"OK, so what is it?"

"You'll have to look."

"Where?"

"Right in the middle. You have to get down on your hands and knees."

Finn stood, arms folded, trying to read their faces. They were terrible tricksters, the pair of them, quite capable of anything. But their expressions were different now. Serious and concentrated.

"Aidie found it," Conn said, wriggling down and getting covered in sand.

"Yes, but what *is* it?"

"A bone. In there." His small finger pointed.

She squatted down as far as she could go without getting plastered. The sand was wet and clinging. Water pooled where the tower of rocks sank into it. Little fish showed silver. Shrimps, almost transparent in the clear water, darted for the safety of floating fronds of black weed. Finn peered past the crusting of barnacles and limpets, the dark jelly clots of sea anemones, still wondering exactly what she was supposed to be looking at.

Then she saw it. Trapped within the pile, pinned deep inside where the corner of one rock rested on another. She reached a hand to touch, and then drew it back. It was definitely bone. The wrong shape and consistency to be stone, and drift wood would have been pulverized by the weight of the rock bearing down upon it. Tiny porous holes showed where the casing had been eroded from the knobbly base. It was covered in a thin layer of slimy green algae. The slender shaft ended in a slanting, uneven break; the jagged point and splintered edges worn smooth by the endless action of the sea.

"We reckon it's a leg bone," Conn said quietly. "Snapped off about here." He indicated seven or eight inches above his sandy ankle.

"Yeah," Aidan breathed, leaning over their shoulders. "It must have belonged to a pirate, or a smuggler, someone like that."

"Yeah!" Conn's eyes were shining. "We reckon there could be treasure!"

"Yeah?" Finn prepared to withdraw. "And it could just as easily be from some kind of animal. A cow, or—"

Conn shook his head violently, spattering her with water and sand. "Don't be stupid! It's much too small!"

". . .or sheep, or something like that."

"Umm, I suppose," Conn's lower lip stuck out, "but

we don't think so." He stood up. "I told you it was no use showing her. Come on, Aidie. Oh, hi!" His voice changed, switching from resentment back to excitement again. "Are those for us? Hey! Cool!"

Finn got to her feet, brushing the sand from her knees, to find Mike Treherne standing behind her.

"Yeah, here." He let the body boards he'd been carrying drop to the sand. He was stripped for beach action, wearing long surfer shorts. "What are you all looking at?"

Finn stood, arms folded, while Conn and Aidie scrambled around, showing Mike the precious bone that they had found. She expected him to rubbish their theory, dismissing it as childish fantasy, like any sensible person. But he didn't do that. He took it seriously.

"It's possible." He stood up, dusting sand from his tanned legs. "More than possible."

"See!" Her brothers grinned up at her, triumphant.

"Oh," Finn frowned sceptically. "How's that?"

"Might not look it, but this coast is dangerous," Mike replied, his blue eyes taking in the length of the shoreline. "Over the years, over the centuries, ships were wrecked here on a regular basis. See out there," he stared out to sea, pointing towards the horizon.

"What? See what?" Conn and Aidan were jostling each other, following the line of his arm.

He indicated a spot out from the shore where whitewater broke round rocks showing just above the surface

"That's where they foundered. That's the Vipers."

The twin black columns were aptly named. Pointed and backward curving, they stuck up like blunt fangs against the sea's sequin dazzle.

"Couldn't ships avoid them? Steer round them?" Finn asked.

Mike smiled at her naiveté. "There's a reef, just below the water, spreading all around them." He demonstrated with outstretched arms. "In towards the shore and over to the headland." He squatted down, gathering flat stones, arranging them, thin edges uppermost, in overlapping ranks. "The rocks are set in ridges, like sharks' teeth. Any ship hitting them will be caught like this." He took a piece of driftwood, pushing it across the top. The sharp edged stones made it hard to pull back. "Rip the bottom right out. It's a hazard to shipping even now. In the days before navigation aids there were some dreadful wrecks here, terrible loss of life. All the little bays chock full of bodies." He stood up, brushing the sand from his hands. "The bone could well be human. It's a distinct possibility."

He caught hold of a pendant he wore, twisting it round on its thin leather thong, and smiled down at Finn, in a way she thought distinctly patronizing. Conn and Aidan were sidling up to him. Finn looked down at the sand. She did not enjoy being smirked at by her brothers.

"That was a long time ago. Ancient history." She countered. "Wooden sailing ships and all that."

"Not so long," he smiled wider, wondering how he

had riled her. "You've seen *Titanic* and that was just ice. Imagine the damage rocks can do. Open up a steel hull just like a can opener. Out there is a kind of crossroads. Always been busy with ships, heading up to Liverpool, or down the Bristol Channel. Even now it's a well-used water way. Danford Haven is one of the deepest harbours in Europe. That's why the ferry terminal's here, and the tankers."

He pointed north to where the oil refineries lay. The jutting headland obscured them from here, but the flares were visible for miles around.

"The approaches are dangerous, though, so the Vipers can still pose a problem. Imagine what it was like in the old sailing days with the weather blowing up from the west and a captain left with no choice but to run for port. And back in those days, the Vipers weren't the only things a sailor had to worry about."

"How do you mean?"

"There were the wreckers." Mike looked from one to another, assessing the impact that the word would have.

"Wreckers?" Conn stared at him, brown eyes shining. They sounded even more exciting than smugglers.

"It's not such a problem now, of course, but back in those days the wreckers would wait for a stormy night, and they'd put out false lights. Tie lanterns to a donkey, or a pony, and walk them up and down. Sailors out at sea would see the bobbing light and think they were following another ship, or looking at craft safe in harbour. They would follow the light

23

straight on to the rocks. The wreckers would be down in the morning to find what the sea had brought them. Saw a wreck as bounty. Everything free for the taking. *Gwyr y bwelli bach*, they called them: the men with the little hatchets."

"Why?"

"They carried short-handled hatchets as the tool of their trade. One side a blade, the other a hook. They used them to pry open barrels, packing cases, chop into wood, and other things, too."

"Like what?"

"Well." He looked from Aidan to Conn, he'd really got them now. "In those days people believed that if there were no survivors, then a wreck and its cargo belonged to anybody who could haul the stuff away. So. . ." He made a chopping gesture with the side of his hand. "They made sure there were no survivors. They killed any that they found and then robbed them of their money or valuables. The dead, too. The hatchets were used to rip out earrings, chop off fingers to get rings, hands to get bracelets."

"That's horrible!" Finn wrinkled her nose.

"Shut up, Finn!" Aidan turned on her. "It's interesting!"

"Why would they do such awful things?" Finn persisted, ignoring him.

"Folks round here were very poor back then," Mike grinned. "No tourists."

"So the bone, *my* bone, could belong to one of their victims?" Conn breathed. What Mike was telling them made his discovery even more fascinating.

"I'm getting to that. The corpses would be collected up right here on the beach and buried between the tide lines in a great big pit."

"Why not in the churchyard?"

"Because people believed that they had to be in reach of the sea. Lest they wander." He made his voice deep and spooky, sweeping down nearer to Conn. "In case the sea came back to claim them—"

"Shut up, will you!" Finn was nearly shouting. "You'll give them nightmares!"

Mike was silenced by her interruption. He turned to the boys with a *what-did-I-do?* look. Conn's sigh and rolling eyes said, "Take no notice." Aidan shrugged and screwed a finger into the side of his head.

The tide was coming back; small cold surges sucking the sand from under their feet. The water trickled and gurgled through the gaps in the rocks piled in front of them. The bone, human, or other, was fast disappearing.

Finn turned to go. They were all getting on her nerves, particularly Mike Treherne. Not only was he Mr Outdoors-Good-At-Everything but he was turning into a know-it-all as well. She couldn't stand the way the boys were looking at him, staring up like a pair of adoring puppies. They'd be gambolling next and doing tricks for biscuits.

Finn began walking up the beach away from them. She shivered, hugging her arms tightly to her. She didn't care what they thought, she'd had enough of them and the beach. It was turning cold, anyway. A little wind seemed to have blown up from nowhere. She rubbed at the goosebumps that had suddenly spread all over her. She knew that it would not be her brothers who would suffer from nightmares.

Chapter Four

Finn was right. The sea came for her again and again that night. But this time the dreams were different, shot through with new horror.

Below the boom of the surf she seems to hear voices calling; the howl of the wind seems laced with human screams. The beach is dark. It is night time. The black water rises and falls, glittering in the pale moonlight. Great wooden spars, splintered and snapped like matches, lie strewn across the sand. There is no sign of a ship out in the darkness, but wreckage floats on the hissing scum of bubbling foam. Dragged back and thrown down again further up the beach, and further, all the time getting nearer, until she can make out individual things among the jumble of floating cargo. Things she took, at first, to be bundles of ragged clothes. Then she sees limbs extended. The flesh is torn, shredded back to bone.

Finn stares, eyes wide, transfixed and paralyzed. The shapeless tumbled bundles begin to move. They are dragging themselves upright, grouping together, moving up the beach towards her. They are near enough for her to see the dripping seaweed-tangled hair, make out the features in ravaged ruined faces, smell the rank fishy stench of decay and salt water.

She runs, fleeing up the beach and away from them. Every now and then, she looks back. Each time they seem closer. They are definitely getting nearer. She turns to run again, dragging herself across acres of thick sodden sand. Her legs are heavy with exhaustion. The sand is sucking at her feet, holding her back, grabbing at her ankles like soft wet hands. She runs on towards the distant breakwater, knowing she isn't going to make it. She stumbles, once, twice, and looks up to see hands reaching down towards her, spread starfish white against the blackness. . .

She fights to get away, her whole body bucking, jerking her to wakefulness.

At least, she thought it was that which woke her. Then she heard a noise, a loud rattling. She sat up in bed, breathing harsh and shallow, sweat breaking out all over as she listened, eyes wide open, trying to sort out what was dream from what was real, trying to identify the sound. The rattle was followed by a bang and then another, loud enough to make Finn jump. She was not dreaming now. Her terror lasted a heartbeat longer, then she relaxed, sighing with relief as she identified the sound. It was the storm-porch door. The catch needed fixing. Mum had noticed this morning and it was on Mike's list of jobs. The wind must have worried it open, banging it back on its frame and shut again.

Finn couldn't be bothered to go down and secure it.

She was too warm and cosy under the duvet. It was not the main door into the house and the wind had died down now. It can wait till morning, she thought, before drowsing off to sleep again.

In the morning, the wind had died down completely. The day was calm and the little patch of sky that Finn could see from her window was as blue as the day before. She lay there for a while, surfacing slowly. From the front of the house came the sound of men's voices, accompanied by metal banging and clanging. Downstairs she could hear her mum yelling. She got out of bed and dragged on yesterday's jeans and shirt to go and see what was happening.

"Come here, you two." Mum was standing in the storm porch shouting to Conn and Aidan who were just finishing their breakfast.

"What is it, Mum?" Conn came out, wiping off his milk moustache.

"What's all this?" Maggie Logan pointed to something dangling from the porch door.

"What's all what?" Aidan was beside his brother.

"This. I won't have you carting stuff up from the beach to rot all over the place. There will be enough of a mess with all these workmen traipsing about." She sniffed, nostrils flaring. "It's already stinking the place out."

Aidan and Conn sniffed too, noses wrinkling. There was a definite whiff in the confined space of the storm-porch, a fishy seaweedy pong.

"It's not me," Conn said quickly, thinking about the stiff, grey sport socks that lived in his wellies.

"Nor me," Aidan agreed automatically. Then he shrugged and looked at his mother. "I don't know what you're on about."

"This! What do you think it is? Scotch mist? I just grabbed hold of it." She wiped her hand on her shirt with a shudder of disgust. "It gave me quite a shock."

"Hey! Watch who you're pushing!"

Finn elbowed Conn out of the way to see what all the fuss was about.

"What's up, Mum?"

"It's these two," Maggie Logan sighed. "Carting I don't know what up from the beach. Look." She pointed to a length of seaweed tied round the handle of the door. "If they want to know what the weather's like, they can watch the forecast, like everybody else."

"We didn't. . ."

"We never. . ."

"It's the wrong kind of weed for that." Mike came up from the yard to see what they were all looking at. "You want bladderwrack. You know, the kind that looks like bubblewrap? This is kelp. It grows in much deeper water. It's still wet. . ." he said, touching the shining brown surface, testing the tackiness between finger and thumb. "Tied in a bowline." He pronounced it bo'lin. "See?" He unwound the length from the door-knob and looped it round his own wrist. "A sailor's knot."

"Hey! Cool!" Aidan and Conn crowded round him. "Can you do knots?"

"Yes," Mike laughed. "Some."

"Will you teach us?"

"Sure."

"Now hang on a minute." Maggie could feel the situation sliding away from her. "Before you three get all Boy Scouty, I still want to know how it got there."

"I dunno, Mum," Conn shrugged. "It wasn't me."

"Me, either," Aidan shrugged, palms out.

"Maybe it was a prank. A joke," Mike suggested. "Someone walking past."

"Like who? No one lives anywhere near, except Mr Griffiths."

Mr Griffiths was their nearest neighbour. He lived up the hill from them and none of them had seen him yet. At the mention of his name, Mike's face changed. His smile remained intact, but his eyes went positively wintry.

"Maybe." Mike undid the kelp from his wrist, doubling it up and snapping it. "But practical joking, joking of any kind, isn't exactly his style. Could be one of the boys coming back from the harbour."

"But why?"

Mike shrugged with the same open-palmed "search me" gesture as Aidan.

"We'll probably never know." Conn took the length of kelp, whirling it round his head and letting it go. It flew end over end, writhing in the air like a snake. "Now can we finish our breakfast?"

"Oi, Mike, boy. You're wanted." A man came round the corner, dressed in brace-and-bib overalls. He was tall, spare, with a thick shock of yellow hair streaked and flecked with grey. "We're about ready to start and I'm not paying you to stand around gossiping."

His smile was warm and friendly, despite his words, but the eyes, the same blue as Mike's, were shrewd and sharp, permanently narrowed in a face weathered and tanned by work outside all the time.

Maggie Logan stepped forward. "It's my fault, Mr Treherne. I've been keeping him talking, I'm so sorry. . ."

"Oh." Mr Treherne looked sheepish now, almost shy. "Didn't see you there, Mrs Logan." He thrust out a huge hand to shake hers. "Call me Jack, Mr Treherne is a bit too formal, like. I'd be wondering who you're talking about."

"In that case, Jack," she smiled, green eyes gazing up at him. She pushed curling wisps of auburn hair back from her face. "I'm Maggie. I don't know if you've met my children?"

She introduced them each in turn, and he shook their hands. His palm and fingers were so callused and fissured and scarred that it was like shaking a handful of razor shells.

"Unusual names."

"Hers is really Fionuala," Aidan said as Finn glared at him. Mike's eyes widened and Conn sniggered.

"I see," Jack Treherne smiled. "The children of Lir."

"Yes," Maggie smiled, reddening slightly. "How did you know?"

"I'm not just a rough old builder, you know." His grin

broadened as her blush deepened. "I was over in Ireland for a while and I like the old tales. Are you Irish, yourself? I thought you might be, what with your colouring and the girl's. . ."

"No," Maggie laughed and shook her head, more hair escaping. "Just romantic. I loved the names, you see. And, of course, the story."

"What is the story?" Mike asked.

"I'm sure the young lady here will tell you some time," Jack Treherne winked at Finn, "if you ask her nicely. Meanwhile we've got scaffolding to get up." He turned to Maggie. "Some of the slates have slipped. If we don't do it now, the winter gales could have the lot off."

"Feel free," Maggie shrugged. "Carole said do whatever and she's paying for it."

"This door needs fixing," Finn reminded her mother.

"Oh?" Jack examined the hinges and tested the catch.

"Yeah," Finn went on. "It bangs when the wind catches it. Kept me awake half last night."

"Did it now?" He looked at her, his thick eyebrows raised in question. "And it was calm last night. Hardly a breath of wind. Well, we can't have that. Mike'll have it fixed in a jiffy, won't you, boy?"

Chapter Five

Mike went to collect his tools and began working on the porch door. Finn watched him for a while through the kitchen window as he chiselled out the rotten wood and cut lengths of new.

"Sure you can manage that?" She came out of the kitchen for a closer look.

"Course." He swore as the chisel slipped.

Finn laughed. "Are you certain?"

"Positive." Mike readjusted his grip and began again. "But I get on better without people looking at me." He levered away a piece of splintering wood. "Carpentry is not a spectator activity."

"Please yourself," Finn shrugged. "I only came out to see if you wanted a cup of tea."

She'd gone by the time he raised his head again.

"Thanks, I'd love one." He muttered to the door jamb. He had been going to ask her to help him as well. He needed someone to hold the door steady while he screwed in the hinges. Well, he wasn't going to ask her now. He'd do it all on his own. Show her. The snooty, stuck up. . . He gave the chisel an extra-vicious thump.

*

He'd finished by the time Finn came out again. She inspected his work, manipulating the door back and forth. The new lock was neatly fitted, and the door worked perfectly, not jamming, or catching. She had to admit that he'd done a good job.

"Does it get your stamp of approval?" He was sitting on the wall of the yard outside, pouring coffee from his thermos.

"I suppose so. It looks all right. We'll have to see if it bangs in the night."

She picked up a lounger and began to manhandle it out of the storm porch.

He stood up. "Need a hand with that?"

"I can manage, thank you," she replied, although it was heavier than she'd anticipated and was pulling her over sideways.

"Where are you off to?"

"Down the garden."

"Sunbathing, is it? All right for some."

Finn glared at him.

"*Sure* you can manage?" He grinned as the lounger began to unfold itself, catching her across the legs.

"I said so, didn't I? Anyway," she stared pointedly at the half-drunk coffee, "I wouldn't dream of keeping you from your work. I'm sure you must have lots of other little carpentry tasks to perform."

Finn hauled her ungainly burden off down the path, trying not to drop the book, magazines and suntan cream she had clamped under her other elbow. She skirted a set of crumbly-looking outhouses and stopped to adjust her grip on things before setting off across the rough patch of ground that was called the garden.

Strangled by weeds, starved by suckers, a straggle of roses marked what was left of the flowerbeds. Fuchsias drooped red and blue heads and clumps of grass grew tall, spiked with a bright orange flower that grew like a weed. A couple of old apple trees, bent out of shape by the wind, provided some shade. Finn headed for them.

She had just settled down to flicking through her magazine, when she heard voices. Her mother and Jack Treherne. They were coming out of one of the outhouses.

"It would be marvellous," her mother was saying. "Just perfect."

"It would take a lot of work. It's very old." Jack patted the thick wall. "This part dates way back."

"I know. I can tell. That's why it would be so good." Some of the excitement ebbed from her mother's voice. "Not that it's likely to happen. My sister is hardly going to pay for me to have a studio made. She'll probably make them into holiday cottages."

Jack nodded. "That's the plan." He paused. "I wish her luck. It's been tried before. . ."

"And?" Maggie looked up, alerted by the doubt in his voice.

"Didn't work out. Not these particular buildings, of course. The main house."

"I'd have thought this was the perfect spot."

"It is, in many ways, but there were problems. 'Not a

happy let', that's what they said. Nerys in the pub, her niece told me. She works for *West Wales Cottages*. They had cancellations, people moving out early, demanding alternatives. Wasn't done up then, of course. Griffiths still owned it. He let it after he had that bungalow built. Planned on making a packet but, like I said, that particular little money-making scheme of his didn't work out." Jack dug out crumbling mortar with a callused thumb. "Not that I cared, mind. Bloody delighted, to be honest." He gave a harsh laugh as though not much love was lost between him and this man Griffiths. "But I wouldn't want it happening to your sister. Wouldn't want her throwing good money after bad, like. That wouldn't be right."

"Have you told her?"

Jack shrugged, "I brought up the subject, like, but she doesn't seem the type to listen to gossip and old stories."

Maggie nodded agreement. Carole was very practical. A no-nonsense, hard-headed business woman who had built up her own company from nothing. As sisters, they were very different.

"She'd only get somebody else in."

Jack laughed again. "That was my thinking."

There was a silence between them, Finn thought that they were moving away. Then her mother said, "The old stories? What were they?"

"Oh, they're to do with the house. Its history. Well, like I say, this part's old."

"How old?" Her mother asked.

"Seventeenth century. Maybe earlier." His hand smoothed the rough-hewed stone. "It's all that's left of the old house. The part you're in. That's quite a lot newer."

"You mean that family deserted this lovely old part and left it to ruin? Why would they do that?"

Jack Treherne laughed, a mirthless bark. "They didn't have much choice in the matter. This here was home to the Gruffydd. . ."

The Welsh pronunciation was slightly different, but Maggie recognized the name.

"The same as Mr Griffiths who sold it to my sister?"

"Same family. They've lived in the Salt House for centuries. There was talk when he moved. But he's a strange one. Unpredictable. He'd been away a long time. When he came back, there was trouble."

Jack did not explain what the trouble was, but his open face suddenly clouded and his expression turned grim. His blue eyes looked off into the distance, staring at nothing, their colour fading and changing until they were as grey and bleak as a winter sea.

"Anyway, after that, he didn't stay in the Salt House for long. Had a new bungalow built and let the old house out. When that didn't work, he put it on the market."

The house had been up in Elliot & Patrick's window for a good while. No one local would touch it. It had stood empty for a long time, that's why it needed so much work doing to it now. Jack wasn't going to tell her that, though. He'd probably said enough already.

Griffiths had to wait for someone from outside to come along and he'd had to lower his price. Jack's eyes brightened as he contemplated the other man's misfortune, a smile twitching at the corner of his mouth.

"The house. This old part," Maggie prompted, interrupting Jack's sudden abstraction. "You were telling me about it?"

"Oh, aye, well. . ." He collected himself. "The Griffiths are an old family, been hereabouts for centuries. They were notorious in the area at one time: smuggling, piracy, wrecking – I don't know what. They lived here, in the Salt House."

"An unusual name. I meant to ask you. . ."

Jack laughed. "No mystery there. They made salt. Channelling the water in from the sea, storing it in reservoirs, probably still there, under the garden. The water was heated until it evaporated, leaving the salt behind. The sea was nearer in them days, before they built the harbour. The salt-making was just a cover, mind, a cover for other activities. You can see the evidence," he ran his callused forefinger down the fine silvered grain of the old door frame. "See that? It's oak that is. See how it curves? Made from old ships' timbers. There's plenty more here, and in the new house, and other houses round about – built with plunder from the sea."

"Aidan and Conn were telling me about that. Something they found on the beach. . ."

"Wrecking was common hereabouts, and the Griffiths were in the thick of it. Got wealthy on it, rich enough to build this house. It was very fine in its day, fortified and everything, just like the gentry."

"So, what happened?"

"Well, one night a big storm blew up, one of the worst ever seen on the coast. This house was nearer the sea then, like I said, and some time during the night great waves came up, sweeping over the place, near enough washing it away. The family took refuge in the cellars, and that's where they were found, every one of them drowned: man, woman and child. Some say the sea came to claim them. Some say it was more than that. . ."

"Oh, like what?"

"Well, they were found down in the cellar, see? Bobbing about among the barrels and contraband, wound around with seaweed, their mouths stopped with sand. Now, a cellar is not a safe place to be, not in a flood, like, and the bolt was shot from the inside. It was as if, as if they'd gone down there to get away, as if they were *hiding* from something. There was talk of a black schooner out in the bay, riding the storm as if it was a fair summer's day. No sign of it in the morning. No wreckage on the shore. Nothing." He shook his head and lowered his voice, as if to speak of such things still held danger. "Some say more than the *sea* came up to claim them."

Maggie shivered slightly as if a cloud had crossed the sun.

"Gosh," she said, rubbing her arms under the sleeves of her summer dress. "That is a powerful story. So they abandoned this house?"

"Yes. Built a new one. No one has lived in this bit here, from that day to this."

"If they were all drowned, how was there anyone left to carry on?"

"The master, old Gruffydd, Gruffydd Ddu they called him – Black Griffiths. They say he was away from home setting false lights, up on the headland, to lure in the shipping. Others say that he had no need of them, that he was up to other business."

"How do you mean?"

"He had a reputation."

"What as?"

"A conjurer, they used to call them hereabouts. A cunning man. An enchanter with the power to call in ships and call up storms. Whatever powers he had, did him no good that night. He came back to find his family as dead as the poor devils they'd despatched with their little hatchets. Some say it was retribution, a judgement. Didn't change him, mind. He carried on, and others after him, until the law put a stop to it."

"When was that?"

"Long ago. Wrecks didn't end. This is a treacherous coast, always will be, but coastguards and navigation aids put the wreckers out of business. Just old stories now."

"Pretty potent ones." Maggie shivered again. "It's a wonder there aren't ghosts!"

Jack guffawed, hoping that his laughter would prove that such ideas were nonsense. He liked her and her kids, did not want to alarm her, or see her leave, neither did he want her to think that they were all a bunch of superstitious peasants down here. He himself dismissed it, but there were stories, recent ones at that, to do with this house and what had happened here. People staying here did not rest easy. That's what they said in the village.

It had begun a couple of years ago, right about the time Griffiths was excavating the *Anna Marie*. Had no business disturbing it, that's what the village said, no good would come of it. Stirring up the dead, disturbing their rest, would cause them to come from the sea and do the same to the living, that's what was said. Not that Jack believed it, but some took Griffiths vacating the premises as proof enough.

"No ghosts, don't worry," he said, smiling to reassure her. "I better be getting back," he added. "See how my lads are getting on."

Their voices faded as they rounded the side of the house. Finn closed her eyes but, disturbed by what Jack Treherne had said about the house, she found it hard to settle. Jack's workmen were getting busy around this side now. She looked up at the house half-encased in its scaffold shell, not at all sure she wanted to stay in a place with such a dark history.

Chapter Six

It was hot under the trees, and airless; Finn found herself plagued by clouds of insects. She gathered her things and prepared to go back to the house.

Mum and the boys were out. Jack and his men had knocked off for lunch. There appeared to be no one about.

Finn wandered round, going from room to room, but there was nowhere she wanted to settle. The thick stone walls made the house cold. This had been a relief when she first came in from the heat outside, but now it was giving her goosebumps. She found herself back in the kitchen and looked in the fridge, but there was nothing she wanted to eat. She wondered where Mum and the boys were. The car was still in the yard, so they were probably down by the sea. As any normal person on holiday would be on a day like this. The cold quiet of the house was making her feel uncomfortable. Finn grabbed her mat and towel and headed down to the beach.

She couldn't see anyone. Maybe they had gone for a walk across the dunes. The boys liked sliding down the slopes and Mum liked drawing the marram grass.

Someone had laid down old railway sleepers to make a path. She was just about to step on to them when someone called her name.

It was Mike. He was sitting on the harbour wall eating his sandwiches.

"Do you want some? I've got stacks. Mam packs enough for an army."

Finn was about to refuse when she realized she was hungry. She accepted one with thanks, even though it was cheese and pickle. *Not* her favourite.

"How about a drink?" He reached in a cool bag and brought out a can of coke.

"How well equipped. I didn't know workmen carried their lunch about in dinky little cool bags."

He swept the can out of her reach. "Do you want it or not?"

"Yes." She held out her hand. She was thirsty.

"Yes what?"

"Pardon?" She had no idea what he was talking about.

"Yes – what?" He repeated slowly, dangling the can.

"Oh. I see what you mean. Yes, *please*!"

"That's better." He handed it to her. "I wanted to ask you something."

"What?"

"Are all English girls as rude as you?"

Finn was taking a swig of coke. His question nearly made her choke.

"Have I been? I didn't mean to be." She mumbled over the rim of the can.

"That's OK. Apology accepted." Mike threw a crust to a gathering gang of gulls. "There's another thing I wanted to know."

"Fire away." Finn hadn't meant her previous remark as an apology exactly, but she let that go.

"Your name. Children of Lir. What's that about?" Mike took a swig from his own can.

"Oh, just Mum being romantic. Dad thought it was silly." Finn's eyes grew distant. "Because we're not Irish, had no connection. It didn't make any sense to him. It started with me, then she went on to name Aidan and Conn. Dad thought she was mad. Maybe she is, in a way. They are very different. That's why they couldn't get on eventually. What do they call it? Irreconcilable differences?" Finn sighed, her voice tailing off.

"And the Children of Lir?" Mike prompted.

"Oh, right," Finn nodded. "Went off the point a bit, there. I'm sorry. Well, it's one of those stories where the wicked stepmother puts a spell on the kids to spite the doting father. In this case she turns them into swans to haunt the rivers and seas of Ireland for ever, singing beautiful songs." Finn laughed. "It's strictly names only. Don't go looking for anything else. The boys sing like a pair of frogs and I hate the sea."

"Nice to be named after characters in a story, though. Nice idea."

"Yes, I suppose."

Neither of them spoke for a while, then Mike said, "Yesterday. When we met and I asked about your dad.

I thought maybe I'd hit a sore spot. If I did, I didn't mean to—"

"It's not that," Finn cut in. "It's not, anyway. A sore spot, I mean." She stared out at the sea. "It's not an issue at all. Not any more. We still see him. It's all very civilized in that way. He's married again. His wife is younger than him. They're expecting a baby. . ."

It certainly had been an issue. They had all been affected in different ways. Mum most, of course, then Conn. He still pined for Dad, although he never let on. Aidan to a lesser extent. Conn had been Dad's favourite. And her. At the time, she'd wanted him to go, wanted the rows to end and to be rid of him. But when he did, the house had an empty feeling. She found herself missing things she'd never even noticed, like his shaving stuff in the bathroom, his briefcase in the hall. And around the time he left, that's when the dreams started again. She could have told Mike all that, but she didn't. She'd never told anyone, not even her best friend. She wasn't about to start discussing it all now with someone she hardly knew.

"I didn't mean to pry," Mike said. "I just didn't want to start off on the wrong foot, that's all."

"And what foot would that be?" Her eyes narrowed on him. "If you don't mean to pry, then don't. Which part of that do you not understand?"

"Sorry. I just thought that's why you were being funny with me."

"Funny? Have I been? I'm sorry." Finn slipped down

from the wall, scattering the gulls. "I'm off to find Mum and the boys. Thanks for the sandwich."

What was it with her? He shook his head as she walked away from him up the beach. She was attractive all right. The swim suit and high-cut shorts she wore showed off her long legs and slim figure, but she had a temperament to go with the tumbling red hair, and those blue-green eyes had a way of changing like the sea: from almost warm to bone-freezingly icy. Sometimes she looked at him like he'd just crawled out from under something. Like he was hired help. Which he supposed he was. He aimed the rest of his sandwich at the posse of gulls sidling up the wall again, hoping to hit the fattest one. He missed and the bread disappeared into a squabbling mass of pecking heads.

He was on his way back to work when he heard her shout. Her voice came from the direction of the dunes, carrying and clear.

"Hey! Stop that! Stop it!"

Mike ran into the sand dunes and nearly collided with a man coming towards him on the same path. He was tall, swarthy-complexioned, with hooded eyes and a drooping moustache. Longish black hair, swept straight back, straggled over the corduroy collar of a long waxed coat. Two big, long-haired lurcher dogs loped along by his side, their pink tongues lolling between serrated rows of teeth. The man looked straight at Mike, black eyes flicking over him, but he gave no sign of recognition. He just marched straight on, hands thrust in pockets, making no apology, even though Mike had to swerve aside to let him past.

"What's happened?"

Mike reached where Finn was standing, her arms folded, shoulders hunched and shaking. He thought she was crying, but when she turned round her blue eyes were blazing fury.

"Did you see!"

"See what?"

"That man and his dogs." She gestured towards the path and then pointed down to the ground, her arm trembling. "Look what they've done!"

A limp furry bundle lay huddled in the sand.

"Is it dead?"

"Of course it is! Those dogs were playing tug of war with it!" She shuddered. "He just stood there watching them. And when I shouted he – he just *laughed* at me."

Mike squatted down. The rabbit was well chewed up. Its fur torn; its body all mauled about. He dug with his hands, scooping a shallow grave in the soft sand.

"Who is he, anyway?" Finn asked as he kicked the dirt back. "He should have those dogs under control. I *hate* people like that."

"That's Griffiths," Mike said, as if that explained everything.

"The one who owned the house we're living in?"

"The very same. How'd you know about that?"

"I heard your uncle telling Mum about it," Finn said as they made their way back towards the house. "The history and that, about the wreckers. Were your family wreckers, too?"

"What? Good God, no." He looked away, jaw tightening, as if she had insulted him. "We certainly were not. The Trehernes were sailors and fishermen. Could have been one of us washed up, couldn't it? We had nothing to do with it. Or the Griffiths family, then or now."

"Family feud?" Finn remarked, remembering Mike's uncle's reaction.

"Something like that." His pace quickened. She could hardly keep up with him. "I've got work to do. Catch you later."

He strode on to the house, leaving her standing. It was her turn to have hit a nerve.

"You haven't seen the boys, have you?" Maggie Logan asked from the sitting-room door.

"Not for a while." Finn was lying on the settee watching TV. "They were in earlier, then they went out again."

"I'm about to get tea ready and there's no sign of them. I have a feeling they might have gone down to the beach. I really don't like them going down there on their own. Mike said he'd keep an eye on them, but he has his own things to do." Maggie Logan bit her lip. "I hope they're not up to something."

Finn hoped so as well, but with those two it was a distinct possibility.

"You want me to go and look for them?" She stood up.

"That would be a big help, thanks Finn. I'd go myself, but I want to get on in the kitchen."

Mike was down at the harbour, helping a couple of fishermen load pots into their crabbing boat. None of them had seen her brothers.

"We've been here a while," Mike said. "We'd have seen them if they'd come to the beach. Have you tried the dunes?"

Finn squinted the way he was pointing. The dunes stretched away like a mini Sahara. She wasn't about to trog all over there. They went on for miles.

"They'll turn up," she said with a shrug. "They always do, worse luck. It's just Mum, she tends to fuss too much."

"Over-protective?"

"You just might say that." She looked down into the harbour, scanning the jostling craft. "Which one's yours?"

Mike pointed out the *Little Jenny*.

"It's very small," Finn commented doubtfully. "Are you sure it's safe?"

"Course it is!" Mike laughed. "You never been sailing, then?"

Finn shook her head. No. And she didn't intend to start now.

"That's more my kind of thing." Finn pointed to a big white motor-cruiser riding next to his little dinghy. "Sunbathing on the back of that. It's a monster! It looks like it ought to be at Cannes, or somewhere." Finn surveyed the sleek, powerful-looking craft. "I don't know anything about boats, but that must have cost a packet."

"Yeah, it did. That's the *Anna Marie 2*." Mike's eyes narrowed. "Belongs to Griffiths."

At the man's name, the two fishermen looked up. One muttered something under his breath, the other one spat into the water.

"What happened to *Anna Marie 1*?" Finn asked.

Mike looked at her sharply to see if she was taking the mickey again. He'd taken about as much as he was going to from her. But the question seemed innocent enough. After all, how could she know?

"It's the name of a wreck," he said quietly. "Griffiths had a hand in excavating it. That's where he made his packet."

Mike directed his gaze down into the harbour. Griffiths' boat was by far the largest craft among the dinghies and little fishing boats. It rode next to them like a swan among a lot of scruffy little ducks and big bellied geese. He did not say any more, and Finn sensed an abrupt change in him. One of the fishermen shouted something, but he did not answer. His bantering mood had gone, replaced by something much darker. He just nodded down at the man and cast the rope off.

"Aidan and Conn aren't down here," he said as the little boat chugged out of the harbour. "Haven't seen 'em. Sorry."

He turned away, effectively dismissing her, and went back to stacking crab pots.

*

The boys were there when Finn got back to the house. They were a bit subdued, especially Conn, but safe and sound, no harm done. Finn's thoughts swung back to Mike. What was all that with Griffiths? Why had Mike got so touchy about him and his boat? Maybe it was jealousy. Maybe he coveted the monster cruiser, would rather have that than his own little dinghy; but somehow Mike didn't seem the kind of person for that. Anyway, it wasn't just him, there was his Uncle Jack. The Griffiths name brought on a sharp mood change in both of them. She sensed an animosity between the two families that stretched way back: deep currents of hatred flowed between them, almost as strong now as in the distant past.

The people here were as deceptive as the sea by which they lived. They might *seem* friendly enough, but some subjects were not to be discussed. Secrets lay just beneath the surface, like hidden reefs.

Chapter Seven

That night, Finn dreamt that it was already morning. Sounds came from outside her window: tap, tap, tap, like metal tools clinking on the scaffolding. Voices talking. Wood creaking, shifting under the weight of feet tramping on the walkways, climbing up the ladders. The men were already here. Sounds came from above. A kind of slithering. The work on the roof was starting. She opened her eyes. Her curtains were apart. She sat up quickly, thinking that she'd over-slept, alarmed that the men might see her in bed. But the sky was still dark outside. How could that be?

All sounds stopped immediately. It must be one of those dreams again: the ones where you think that you're awake, but in fact you're still asleep. Yes, that was it. What she heard was probably the wind in the scaffolding. A rope, or something, banging against metal. . .

As if to confirm her thinking, there was a quick burst, then another, a kind of pattering followed by a spatter of drops hitting the window. It must be raining, although yesterday had been clear right through to the evening. According to Mike and his uncle, the weather here changed very fast, sun one minute, storm the next. So that must be it.

She sat up, pushing her hair back. There it was again, but this time Finn was less sure what to make of it.

The sound was something wet, all right, but more solid than she first thought. Well, not exactly solid, but something with weight behind it, hitting the glass with a steady thunk. What it was, Finn could not guess. Goosebumps rose all the way up her arms and the hair crept on the back of her neck. She sank down in her bed, pulling the cover over her head.

In the morning, sand lay in clotted lumps on the outside window-ledge and scattered across the walkway. Finn crumbled one between finger and thumb. The grains were still wet, sticky and clinging, although the ground below was bone dry and the sky above clear. Again, she heard voices.

Mike and Aidan were sitting on the end of the wooden walkway, legs dangling. She whistled to attract their attention. They looked down and around, unable to locate the sound. So Finn wiped the sand from her hand and whistled again, putting two fingers in her mouth to produce an ear-splitting siren shriek.

"Oh, hi, didn't realize it was you." Mike got up to come to her window.

"You're starting early." The sun had barely risen above the ridge behind the house.

"Have to crack on while the weather's good. Where did you learn to whistle like that?"

"Junior school playground. Kid called Jeremy taught me."

"Well, you better not do it again." He looked at her straight faced. "You'll have the guys off the roof in a minute."

"Why's that?" Aidan gave a little whistle himself and then squinted up at him.

"Lots of them are fishermen."

"So what?"

"They're superstitious. All sailors are." He held a piece of rope, bright blue, a piece of the stuff they used to lash the scaffolding poles on to the lorry. He carried on working it as he spoke. "On boats whistling is considered *very* bad luck. Especially if it's a woman doing it."

"Not surprised. Women are always bad luck." Aidan grinned as Finn glared at him.

"Why would it be unlucky?" She asked, ignoring her brother.

"Because she might whistle up the wind. And we don't need that here, especially when we're working on a roof."

It was hard to tell if he was joking.

"Why a woman?"

"Because she might be a witch."

"They'd be right in your case, then." Aidan said, grin widening. "You walked right into that one."

"Does Mum know you're out here?" Finn asked in her big-sister voice. She'd had enough of him for one morning already.

"She didn't say I couldn't." Aidan's confidence faltered.

Finn laughed, she'd got him now. "That's because she doesn't know. . ." As she looked at Aidan's shifty little face, a new thought hit her. She wondered that she hadn't thought of it before. It was so completely obvious. "I suppose it was you out here last night? Throwing sand and stuff about?"

"Course not." Aidan looked shocked. "I wouldn't come out here at night. I might fall off. I'm not *that* stupid."

"Conn, then. *He's* that stupid." Finn squinted along the scaffolding. "Where is he, anyway?"

"I dunno," Aidan shrugged, but he was looking shifty again. "I'm not his minder."

"It *must* have been one of you."

"It wasn't him, and it wasn't me. I don't know what you're on about, Finn."

"This." Finn pointed down at the scattered clumps of sand.

"That could be off the workmen's boots, or anything!"

"It's not the right kind of sand!" Finn held a handful under his nose. "Their stuff's dark orange and gritty. This is more like sand off the beach. . ."

"So? Somebody probably tramped it up here."

"Yeah. You."

"Not me," Aidan shook his head. "Try again, Finn. I'm not guilty."

"Whatever." Mike toed the little clods to the bone-dry ground below. "He's right. It could've dropped off their boots on the way up to the roof."

"I suppose," Finn conceded reluctantly.

What did it matter to him? He wasn't waking terrified night after night.

Not a good idea to go on about it any more, though. Best to let it ride, bide her time, because if it *was* Conn and Aidie playing tricks, she would get them eventually, then they'd be in *big* trouble. But what if it wasn't them?

"I mean, what else could it be?" Mike was looking at her quizzically.

"Nothing. Doesn't matter. What were you two up to, anyway?" She dusted the sand from her hands. "Before I interrupted you."

"Mike's been showing me how to tie knots." Aidan produced a tangle of string from his pocket. "And he's been telling me stuff."

"Like what?"

"About sea monsters and enchanters, all kinds of interesting stuff. You can call them up by knots!" Aidan held up his own efforts. A grubby length of grannies.

"What?" Finn looked at Mike.

"Not exactly," Mike said sheepishly. "I was just telling him some of the local legends. But you probably wouldn't be interested."

"I might be. Try me."

"You remember the Vipers?" He nodded out to where the sea broke round the jagged black rocks. "One story says that that's the mouth of the *afanc*. A kind of a sea monster, a sea-serpent type thing that lies curled up under the waves with only its head showing. In the old days, it was believed that some people, witches, conjurers, they called them round here, or cunning men, had the power to call up the wind, or call in boats, if they stood on a certain stone, called a cursing stone. The ship would be wrecked on the Vipers to feed the *afanc*."

"Kind of like a sacrifice?"

"Kind of like that, but with benefits. The people on the shore would get what was left. Also, they believed that if they didn't do it, the *afanc* might come after them. It was better to sacrifice strangers than put your own at risk. Of course, it's just old stories. . ." Mike stared, eyes narrowed against the glare. "It is strange out there, mind. Local fishermen keep well away from the fangs. Apart from obvious reasons, compasses go crazy anywhere near them."

"Tell how they summoned the ships," Aidan prompted. It was his favourite part of the story.

"One way was to have a rope, like this," Mike held the bright blue length stretched between his hands. "Or a piece of cord or string, and tie knots in a line of three. As each knot was loosened, so the wind increased."

"What kind of knots?" Finn asked, curious.

"Ordinary sailors' knots, probably. Maybe a bo'lin, like this, then a figure of eight. Then maybe some kind of stopper." As he spoke, he began forming the last knot. "Something more elaborate, like a Monkey's Fist," he clenched his hand, "which is a knot like this. The first knot would bring a gentle breeze. The second," he pulled, tightening the central knot, "would bring something stronger."

"And the third?" Aidan asked, already knowing the answer.

Mike laced the rope round the fingers of his left hand, pulling the end through to make a clublike knot.

"Freeing the third knot would bring a gale, a storm, a tempest."

"And people believed this?"

"Oh, yes." Mike turned to Finn. "Sailors would buy bits of knotted thread and take them with them on voyages. It was useful to be able to summon the wind, especially on sailing ships. They were probably careful not to undo the last one, though. Here you go," he handed the knotted rope to Aidan. "I better get on. I've got to go to the yard in the pick-up soon." He looked down at the boy. "Do you still want to come?"

"Yeah!"

"What about Conn?"

"I don't know about him. He's in a bit of a mood."

Mike shrugged. Whatever.

"See you later. Don't go messing with the knots, now."

He winked at Aidan and turned away with a smile, but it was still hard to tell if he was joking.

"Do you believe all that stuff?" Aidan asked as Mike climbed the ladder up to the roof.

"Of course not." Finn replied. "What are you doing?"

Aidan was fiddling with the first knot.

"Here," he pushed the free end of the rope up into a loop. "This bit's called the bight. That end goes round like that. . ."

Out to sea, the water seemed to shift and crinkle, changing from blue to green and back again, like iridescent silk. It had been dead calm before, but now the pine trees creaked as the breeze caught their bows, the needles rubbing together in little rushing sounds.

"Stop it!"

"I'm only seeing how he did it!"

"Well, don't."

Finn put her hand out to grab his. She'd never thought herself in the least superstitious, but she'd have taken the rope off him, if he hadn't snatched it away.

"It's mine!" Aidan scowled. "He gave it to me. You're not having it. I want to show it to Conn. Anyway, you said you didn't believe in it! What is your problem?"

Finn shook her head in answer to his question. She hadn't believed that she had one – until now. Maybe she ought to tell someone, about her broken nights, about the unease she felt, but who was there to tell? Mum would only worry and she seemed to really like it here. She seemed happy. Finn did not want to spoil all that. Mum had been through a difficult time since Dad left. Not telling her things had become automatic.

Finn shivered as the chill little wind blowing in from the sea seemed to bring her dreams back. That odd mix of déjà vu and premonition that her dreams had. Something *bad* going to happen.

Chapter Eight

Where *was* Conn?

Aidan had spent all morning with Mike, visiting the yard and riding round in the pick-up. They stopped in a caff on the way back, so he didn't really miss his brother until the afternoon. Conn had been in a funny mood earlier. Now he seemed to have disappeared altogether.

Aidan had shown him the rope Mike had made, even giving it to him to keep, but Conn hadn't been very interested, just stuffed it into his pocket. Aidan had asked if he wanted to come into town with Mike, but Conn had shrugged, saying he had business of his own. Aidan thought he knew what that might be, and knew Conn could get into trouble for it, but he'd let him go anyway. Conn had annoyed him, rejecting his attempts at friendliness. But it was afternoon now, and Conn still wasn't back. Aidan stood in the kitchen, biting his lip. He should never have let him go off on his own. . .

"Have you seen Conn?" he asked Finn as she came in.

"No, I thought he'd gone with you and Mike."

Aidan shook his head.

"He's bound to be somewhere. . ." Finn looked round.

"He didn't go with Mum?"

It was her turn to shake her head.

Aidan didn't say anything more, but he looked worried.

"Where do you think he *might* be?" Finn asked quietly. Aidan was hiding something. She knew the signs. She knew when either one of them was up to something. "You better tell me. Mum'll be back any minute."

"He might – he might have gone up to that man – Mr Griffiths' house."

"Why would he do that?"

"To get his ball back. It's the stitched leather. The one Dad bought. . ."

"Why would Mr Griffiths have it?" Finn sat down.

"Yesterday afternoon – we were in the field next to his house, having a kickabout, when Conn punted it into his garden. We went to have a look for it, but we couldn't find it. We went back after tea, but it was getting dark and the dogs started to bark. Conn said he'd go up in the morning. But he should have been back ages ago."

"OK, OK." Finn stood up. "We'd better go and look for him. Perhaps Mike's seen him. Maybe he can help."

Mike found Conn sitting under the tall pines in the little wood above the house.

"You all right?"

Conn nodded, wiping his face on his sleeve.

"What's the matter?" Mike went down on one knee when he saw that the boy was crying.

"Nothing." Conn sniffed and looked away, embarrassed that Mike had found him in tears. A half-deflated football dangled between his knees.

"Where've you been?"

"Up at Griffiths' house looking for my ball. He didn't catch me. I waited for him to go out. And I didn't go in, or anything," he added quickly. "Just had a nosy through the windows, and that. I found this by the back door," he held up the punctured ball to show the fang marks in the leather panels. "He must have given it to his dogs."

He didn't say any more. Fresh tears threatened.

Mike nodded in sympathy. "He can be nasty like that. Spiteful. One time, he said I'd been messing with his boat, threatened my Dad with a bill for hundreds of pounds. Best to keep away from him."

Conn hung his head, trying to hide that he was crying again.

"It's OK," Mike said quietly. "Finn told me the ball was special. A present from your dad. I had a watch once, a fake Rolex from Thailand. That was special to me. My uncle bought it. . ."

"Jack?"

"No," Mike shook his head. "A different one. He's dead now. Anyway, a kid at school tried to swipe it. I got into a fight about it and somehow the watch got stomped. When that happened, I cried, too, and I was a lot older than you."

Conn looked up at him through his tears. "I bet you gave that kid a bit of a hiding."

"I did, as it happens, but it didn't fix the watch, or how I felt inside. Come on." He stood and reached down to help Conn up. "Tell you what. How would you like to go for a sail? Out on my boat. How'd that be?"

"Yeah," Conn said, sniffing for a last time, the ghost of a smile lighting his eyes. "That sounds all right."

"OK. It's a deal," Mike helped him up. "Here," he gave him a tissue. "Blow your nose."

"Can I come, too?" Aidan asked.

"Of course." Mike turned to Finn. "How about you?"

Finn shook her head.

"Are you sure? I've got all the gear, lifejackets and stuff. And you'll be quite safe with me. I'm a qualified sailing instructor." He looked up. The sky above was blue and clear, there was just enough breeze to ruffle the leaves in the trees. "It's a great day for it."

"No thank you," she said, shaking her head again. Her refusal came out prim and clipped.

Mike shrugged, giving her a lop-sided "suit yourself" grin.

"She's scared, scared of the water." Aidan jeered.

"Yeah, it frightens her." Conn added. Finn's blank refusal had embarrassed them both.

"What's the matter?" Mike asked, comprehension dawning. "Can't you swim?"

Conn and Aidan sniggered.

"It's not a crime. In the old days lots of sailors and fishermen couldn't."

"Why not?"

"Reckoned it wasn't worth it. Reckoned if the sea wanted you, it would have you. You couldn't cheat it. Swimming just meant it took longer to drown. It wasn't until—"

"Well, that's all very interesting," Finn cut in, "but actually I can swim." She was annoyed with the way her brothers were acting, putting her down, sucking up to Mike, giving him an excuse to patronize her. "I'm a good swimmer, if you must know," she added icily. "I've got medals. I learnt in the pool at school."

She didn't mind swimming pools. They were safe. Chlorine and clean. You could see the bottom; you could see the sides; you could see wavy black lines through blueness. There were rails and steps; every so many metres markers showed your depth. The sea was different. It tasted of salt. It went on for ever. Finn shuddered. Bottomless. Horrible.

Mike frowned, unable to understand. Finn shrugged and turned away from his pitying incomprehension. How could she explain? He practically had gills. The original waterboy.

"She doesn't have to come," Mike said to Conn and Aidan. "It'll be a bit of a squeeze anyway."

"When shall we go?" Conn asked, his mood fully restored, tears forgotten.

"How about now?"

"Wow! Cool!"

"How big's your boat?"

"Does it have an engine?"

"Is it hard to sail?"

"Which one is it?"

The boys bombarded Mike with questions as they went down to the harbour.

"That one there," Mike pointed her out. "The *Little Jenny.*"

"Not very big is it?" Conn sounded slightly disappointed.

"It's big enough," Mike grinned. "Just looks small from up here."

"Which one is Griffiths'?"

"The one moored over there," Mike pointed again. "The motor cruiser."

"Hey!" Conn's eyes widened. "That's big!"

Mike nodded, "Unhn."

"Did you really mess with it, like he said?"

Mike lost his smile and his face darkened.

"*I* will," Conn went on. He felt safe with Mike, tough. Brave enough to let his hatred bubble to the surface. "Now I know which one, I'll go down at dead of night and mess it all up. I'll drill holes in the bottom of it. I'll open the plug thing or what ever it is—"

"Sea cock," Mike supplied absently. He was gazing down at the long sleek cruiser floating off the mud with the rising tide. "No, you won't." He shook his head slowly. "You won't do any such thing. You won't go near it." He turned on Conn, his voice serious, his expression stern. "You won't go anywhere near

Griffiths' house, or his boat, or him. Do you understand me?"

Conn swallowed and nodded, tears threatening again at this sudden fierceness. At that moment, he was not sure exactly who he was most afraid of, Mike or Mr Griffiths.

Chapter Nine

Finn did not dislike the sea. From up on the cliffs she could see its beauty. She gazed down, noting the change of colours in the wrinkling surface, the shade darkening from the shore, from pale green aquamarine, through azure, to the dark, almost navy of the open sea. She could appreciate it – from a distance.

It was not that she was afraid – not in the conventional sense. It was like being up here. Finn herself had no terror of heights. She stepped down from the cliff path and descended the shelving slope to stand right on the edge, just to prove it to herself. A few clumps of tough grass clung to the dry crumbling ground beneath her feet – then nothingness. Finn could lean out, peer down the sheer cliff to the cove below, and not feel a flicker of fear, but she understood those who did.

She knew what they felt. She knew exactly why certain people avoid high places. It had nothing to do with thinking you were going to fall off. It was far more complicated than that. The real fear, the absolute terror, came not from dread, but from desire. Certain people would not come up here because they could not trust themselves not to jump. Not to take that last step out.

So it was with Finn and the sea. She could not go out on it, could not go beyond her depth even, because, if she did, she would want to dive and never come back to the surface. To go down and down, floating and floating to the very depths, to join the dead, the drowned.

When Finn was very small, something terrible had happened to her. A Near Death Experience, some would call it. She had been to the brink of death and back again. This was the root of her dreams and her fear, and perhaps other things besides.

So far, on this holiday, she had avoided the memory; thinking about it here would not be safe. But it had come on its own, invited by a random thought, a chance remark, until it finally arrived at the front of her mind. It had happened so long ago that she did not know how much of the story was her own memory, and how much had been supplied by adult recall filling in the details for her.

She had nearly drowned. It was one of her first ever times on a beach, the first she remembered anyway, and she must have been about three. Conn was not born and if Aidan was there then, she had no awareness of him. As soon as she saw the sea, she began to run. She can see herself, a small figure streaking across the sand, in a green swimsuit with white straps and white stripes, red hair streaming behind her like a flag. She reaches the surf curling to shore, but she does not stop, she plunges straight in, diving into the wave, into the weed floating deep inside it. She sees herself, as though from above, her hair floating red in green and purple weed, wrapping round her like a winding sheet.

She does not remember the shock of the water, or not being able to breathe, she remembers only peace, and hands reaching for her. Perhaps it is a trick of memory, perhaps she was disorientated, twisted by the water, perhaps they were coming from above, but she remembers them clearly as coming up from below. Fingers, long and white, stretching from the depths and in the muffled sound of the surf she seems to hear voices calling to her.

Suddenly the brightness of the sun hurts her eyes. The air is full of noise, discordant calls and cries, and she longs to be back under the sea again. She had been comfortable and happy there, but she is being dragged and picked up, snatched back to the world above.

She can see her mother, long summer dress dripping wet, catching round her legs, running up the beach. She is sobbing, features contorted. Her own face lolls white over her mother's arm, eyes shut tight, the skin round her lips blue, like the time she drew on a felt-tip moustache and couldn't wash it off. There is weed caught in her hair: crinkly purple, and bright green like lettuce.

She is on the sand now, laid down. A man is kneeling by her, leaning over her. She can see his back, brown and glistening with water drops. He is wearing swimming trunks, marked with a swirly pattern, orange and black. She cannot see her own face, or what he is doing to her, but suddenly she is coughing and spluttering, looking up at him. He has blue eyes – like Mike. She tastes salt, thick in her mouth and the back of her throat, and is sick in the sand. A sigh goes through the people crowding round. She is picked up, made a fuss of. The incident is over.

What did Mike say? If the sea wants you, it will have you? She cheated it once, but she can feel the call, in the waves, thunder and roar, as the surf whispers to shore. It is as if something is out there waiting for her. Something. Or someone.

Finn shivered and came back to herself. Far safer to be up here, for her and everybody else. She trained the binoculars, scanning the bay for the small craft. Mike and the boys should be visible by now. Sure enough, there they were, tacking their way out of the harbour, sails out, ready to catch whatever breeze there was.

The little boat was doing well, making good speed, cutting through the water, out into the bay. She could see the boys in their brightly coloured lifejackets, moving from one side to the other under Mike's command. Mike was doing most of the work. She could see him leaping about, pulling on this and heaving on that. It looked hard, but they seemed to be having fun. She could just hear their excited shouts, thinned by distance to high gull cries.

Since it was the boys' first time, Mike had promised not to take them too far, and that he would be very, very careful.

Finn was tracking their progress through the binoculars when she suddenly felt a chill; a prickling along the spine. She instinctively glanced behind, and saw a man up on the high cliff path. The ground beneath her was dry and friable. As she turned, small pebbly stones shifted under her pivoting foot and suddenly it was as if she was standing on marbles. She let out a shout, looking round desperately, but there was nothing to hold on to, nothing to save her. Her arms pinwheeled and for one sickening moment she lurched towards emptiness, but her balance was good. She hurled herself landward, jamming her right foot into the slope to stop her slide, and side-stepped her way to safety.

Once on safer ground, she threw herself down, clutching her knee. She had wrenched it in that violent sideways turn and it was beginning to throb. She looked up and noticed that the figure on the cliff was still there. It was Griffiths. She recognized him despite the blurring tears of pain. He had made no attempt to go to her aid. He made no move to see if she was all right. He just stood there, his hand raised, two fingers curled as if in blessing. He stared at her for a moment longer, his mouth curved in an odd lop-sided smile, then he went on his way.

The path Griffiths followed took him round to the point. He walked head down, hands in pockets, as if deep in thought. As he went, he began to whistle a tune to himself, high, thin, monotonous.

He was making his way to *Pentir y Dewin* – the Headland of the Enchanter. Finn found the place on the map in her pack, but the name meant nothing to her. The narrow tongue of land descended in stages to a thin sharp ridge which sloped down into the sea. It formed the righthand point of Yellowstone Cove, which appeared on the map as a penny-sized bite out of the coastline. Finn peered down into it. The name seemed meaningless. The rocks down there were grey and brown just like all the others.

She turned her attention back to the sea, to Mike and her brothers. They were well out from the harbour now. Between them and the open sea lay the Vipers, sticking up like huge jagged teeth, guarding the entrance to the bay.

From up here, it was much easier to see the true extent of the reef. It spread like a dark stain, curving round, extending all the way to the shore in fat black coils. Small waves foamed across rocks which broke the surface in rows like spiny crests. It was easy to see how the local legend had grown up. It did, indeed, look like a giant worm or serpent; some monstrous sea creature curled in readiness just below the waves.

Out in the bay, the sails hung limp on the *Little Jenny*. Mike hauled them in. The wind had dropped to nothing. The breeze, which had been blowing steadily all day, had died right away. The air felt heavy and oppressive. The boat rocked from side to side. Although there was no wind, there was the beginning of an ugly swell. Mike checked the two boys for signs of greenness. If they were prone to seasickness, this kind of movement was sure to bring it on.

The swell had probably been generated by a big ship, a tanker or ferry, on its way into the Haven. There were plenty of them going in and out, and they could constitute a hazard to smaller craft. It was not just a case of being ploughed down. Their giant bow-waves and wakes could seriously upset a little boat like this, even swamp it.

Mike decided to give up on sail. He manhandled the outdoor motor, fitting it over the back. It was cheating a bit, but they would have to rely on good old diesel to take them back. He looked out across the water to where tidal races and powerful currents rippled the surface like tears in silk. Too little wind could be as dangerous as too much. People didn't always realize that. It was risky to be drifting around, entirely at the mercy of sea and tide. Some of the currents here were so strong they would have a much bigger craft than this on the rocks in minutes.

He pulled the starter, waiting for the sudden thick oily smell, the usual juddering throaty response, but nothing happened. The engine coughed and died on him. He had another go. Nothing. He checked the fuel gauge. It showed plenty. He gave it a tap, in case the needle was stuck, but the needle stayed in place. He tried the starter again with a shake of the head. Still nothing.

Mike left the motor and went for the oars. There was still no wind, but a glance to the shore told him that the boat was moving fast. A tidal race had them in its grip and would take them towards the shallowest part of the reef, known locally as the *Dannedd y Ci: The Dog's*

Teeth. Each area of the reef that came above the water had its own name. Here the rocks showed in great serrated rows.

Aidan and Conn carried on joking and messing about: trailing their hands, flicking up water, leaning over the side looking for fish. It was not until Mike told them to grab an oar and row that they began to realize that things were serious. They did as they were told, sobering down quickly. Conn was excited still, and eager, as if this was another part of the adventure. Aidan's enthusiasm was waning. In fact, he was beginning to feel distinctly queasy.

Mike took position at the front, putting them at the back. They pulled together, rowing as hard as they could, but progress was pitiful.

From his place on the Point, Griffiths watched the little boat crawl over the water like a crippled bug. In his hands he held a length of bright blue rope, one knot already unravelled. He found it odd that people would seek to create magic and then carelessly discard it, as if it was a casual curiosity: a joke, a parlour trick, a means of showing off. They did not realize the power contained within. To make a magical object like this, and then leave it just lying about, was irresponsible to say the very least.

He'd found the knotted rope up at his house, under the picture window at the back. At first, he had puzzled how it had got there, mystified as to its purpose. He had rolled the rope carefully, put it in his pocket, and carried on walking round his house. That's when he'd noticed that the football was missing. One of those ginger-haired brats from the Salt House must have come to reclaim his property.

Had a good look round at the same time, no doubt. Griffiths didn't like that. He didn't like people spying about. Probably put up to it by that Treherne boy. Too much of a coward to go himself. Send a kid to do his dirty work. Typical of that family. Sneaking, cheating, underhand lot.

Whatever the ins and outs, they had delivered themselves right into his hands. Griffiths' grip tightened on the smooth nylon ply as he touched the figure of eight, reading the intricacies of the second knot. Nicely done. Neatly accomplished. The Treherne boy again. He was a good sailor, by all accounts. Griffiths' dark face split with a mirthless grin. Time to see just how good.

His fingers began to work the rope, loosening the loops, unmaking the knot. He stood on his high promontory, passing the rope between his fingers like rosary beads, and began to whistle his tuneless tune. Someone had broken the first rule of magic: Don't make a spell unless you intend to use it. A slight breeze ruffled his hair.

Out in the bay, Mike felt the first ghost of a wind against his sweating skin. He shipped the oars and set the sails to catch it before it died again. He held up a wetted finger. The breeze was coming from the west and strengthening. Out beyond the twin black rocks, the sky was dark, the horizon lost in iron-grey, thickened and fuzzy with rain. A squall was coming in from the open sea. They could build out of nowhere, strike without warning.

The wind was reaching to shore now, whipping Finn's hair about, blowing it back from her face. She saw that Griffiths had made his way round the curve of the cliff to the point where it dipped down towards the sea. He stood right on the edge, oblivious of the buffeting the wind was giving him. He held something in his hands, a short length of something blue and flexible, and was staring out to sea. Finn followed his gaze. It was fixed on the *Little Jenny.*

Out in the bay, the boat looked small and fragile, scudding along as frail as a walnut shell. Behind it an angry knotted mass of black cloud had quickly gathered. It was moving off the horizon, coming in towards shore with what seemed like incredible speed, zipping this way and that like some dark, monstrous airborne creature. Thick columns of rain slanted across the sea like fingers searching for the little boat. Finn watched, helpless to do anything, as all the while the waves grew, breaking in bursts of spray as if they were being sucked up into the sky.

Mike flattened sail and fought to stay in control as he ran just ahead of the storm. It would take all his seamanship to get them back to the harbour. Aidan was being sick now, hanging over the side. He was out of the game, but Conn seemed unaffected. Just the opposite. He seemed thoroughly exhilarated. He was proving himself fearless and quick, with a willingness to obey orders that Mike had not expected. He had the makings of a good sailor, but this was his first time out. The responsibility lay with Mike. He'd brought them out here, it was his job to get them back.

He put those concerns out of his mind to concentrate on the sails, the wind and the waves. To make the harbour would be like slotting a ball from the halfway line into a goalmouth shrunk to the size of a door. Shouldn't be *too* difficult. The strong wind and rising sea sent the boat scudding through the foam, skimming over the sea like a stone. This was what sailing was all about. Mike reefed sail and eased the tiller. If it wasn't for the two kids on board, he would be really enjoying himself.

"Phew, that was close!" Mike grinned as he threw a line to Finn.

"Are you two all right?" she called down to her brothers.

They were both soaked to the skin. Aidan looked green but Conn's eyes were shining.

"Mike was brilliant!" Conn called up. "It was amazing. Better than Alton Towers! Better than anything. I can't wait to do it again!" He nudged his brother. "How about you, Aidie?"

Aidan gave a shudder that said never would be too soon. He grasped the metal ladder fixed on to the harbour wall, hands white, arms shaking. Mike steadied him and gave him a push from behind. He made halting progress up to Finn who knelt and reached down for him.

Conn stayed in the well of the boat, unwilling to leave. He looked round, fists curled, his face a shifting mix of awe and delight. Fragile as the little craft was, he felt at home on it. He had found something he would love all his life.

"Kid's a natural," Mike put a hand on his shoulder. "We'd never have got in if it wasn't for him."

Conn went pink at Mike's praise and beamed with pride.

"That's as maybe," Finn frowned, relief that they were all right rapidly being replaced by concern about the consequences of their escapade. "But if Mum finds out, he won't be going paddling, let alone sailing."

"You won't tell her?" Conn looked up in anguish.

Finn thought for a bit. She knew she ought to, but it had turned out OK in the end, and what Mum didn't know wouldn't hurt her.

"She'd only fret. But you'd better get up to the house and out of those wet things. If she asks tell her you fell in a rockpool, or something."

The two boys gave Mike his lifejackets back and squelched back to the house in sopping wet trainers.

"I wonder where that came from?" Finn looked over Mike's head. Out to sea, the sky was blue again. The wind had gone. The sea was dying down. It was as if the day had suddenly tilted and was righting itself.

"Beats me." Mike shrugged. "Just happens. Squall like that come up out of nowhere and there's nothing you can do about it. Nasty while they last, though. Looks like you were right not to come out." He laughed. "You aren't gifted with second sight, by any chance?"

Finn flushed. "Of course not. I told you, I just don't like boats."

"Not the only one in your family." He nodded towards where Aidan had missed the side of the boat. He lowered a bucket over the side. "I better clean that up. Care to join me?"

Finn shook her head. "No thanks. Seriously. What do you think happened?"

"I told you – I don't know. It's just weather."

"You don't think that. . ."

"Think what?"

It was on the tip of her tongue to tell him about Griffiths. The way she was sure that he had made her fall. The way he had stared out to sea with that strange rooted fixity. He seemed almost to conduct the storm, with something bright blue held in his hands like a flexible baton.

She could have said all that, but she did not. What had seemed possible up on the cliff top now seemed foolishness. The first part sounded paranoid, even to her. As for the rest? Mike already thought she was neurotic. She didn't want to compound that by coming over as some New Age nutcase believer in magical superstitions and old wives' tales. Anyway, no one could change the weather just like that. No one could have that kind of power. How could the storm be anything to do with Griffiths?

Chapter Ten

The boys were drenched to the skin. It was hard to disguise from Mum what had happened to them. She wasn't buying any stories about slipping off rocks while looking for crabs. She took one look at Aidan and knew. Falling into rock pools didn't leave people green about the gills. She got the truth out of them and she was adamant: no more sailing, no more boats.

The boys accepted her judgement, Conn with some reluctance, but now he had a new activity in mind. Fishing. He had seen men fishing from the beach as the tide came in, and wanted to have a go himself. Aidan was all for it, too, once he knew that they didn't have to go on a boat again. Mike offered to supply the gear, fishing being another one of his interests, and they knew it would be hard for their mother to refuse. They used to go fishing with Dad.

"It can't do any harm, I suppose," she said finally, "That's if Mike doesn't mind. I don't want you being a nuisance to him. He has his work to do."

"It's fine, Mrs Logan," Mike smiled. "I've been meaning to get a bit of fishing in."

*

The next day Mike's uncle let him knock off early. Now that the roofing was well underway, Mike wasn't really needed. Jack had taken quite a shine to Maggie, and didn't seem bothered about his nephew acting as unofficial minder to her children.

"Keep your lads safe and him from under my feet."

They planned to set off down to the beach in the early afternoon. The tide wasn't right yet for fishing, so Mike had suggested a bait-finding expedition. They were taking buckets to put crabs in. "Crabs are good for bass", and a spade to dig for lugs which were some kind of worm things.

"They're dead rare now," Aidan explained. "But Mike knows where to find 'em."

"He would," Finn said, without looking up from her book.

"Do you want to come?" Aidan had been sent to ask her. He'd found her in the garden.

"Fishing? You've *got* to be joking!"

"We aren't doing that yet," Aidan explained patiently. "It's just like rock-pooling really. You used to like that," he added, remembering other holidays.

"Yeah, well, I don't now. I don't see why I should help you find little creatures to stick on hooks to kill other ones." She shuddered at the thought. It sounded slimy and smelly and disgusting. "Why don't you leave them all alone?"

"OK, if that's how you feel." Aidan hitched his rucksack higher on his shoulder. "Mike asked if you wanted to go, that's all."

"Tell him, thanks, but no." She squinted up at her brother from her lounger. "Why do you need that huge bag?"

"Mum's packed us some sandwiches."

"You've only just had lunch!"

"We might get peckish. And I was reading that there are fossils. . ."

Finn rolled her eyes. Given any kind of expedition, Aidan was the kind of kid who wanted to take everything with him, including the kitchen sink, if anyone would let him. God knows what he had squirrelled away in that bag of his. *She* would have made him leave it all at home. But then, she wasn't in charge. Mike was.

"Rather him than me," she muttered.

"What?" Her brother enquired.

"Nothing." Finn turned her attention back to her book. "Have a nice time."

They set off in a clatter of buckets and spades, the boys chattering, their voices high with excitement, Mike's deeper and different, his accent soft and distinctive. Perhaps she should have gone with them. Finn suddenly felt a pang of doubt, a sharp feeling of being left out.

She located her place in her book again, but found it hard to settle. The noise from the roof-work was incessant: the slither and crash of falling tiles punctuated by hammering and shouting. In the end she was forced to find refuge inside.

Her mother was sitting at the kitchen table having a cup of tea with Jack.

"Why don't you go up to your room?" She suggested when Finn started complaining.

Finn made a face. It was even worse inside the house. Every little sound reverberated down from the rafters. It was like being inside a drum kit.

"There'll be men tramping up and down outside my window."

"Well, go for a walk, then." Maggie's tone verged on exasperation. "Find the others. You've been lying about all day. The exercise will do you good."

"I don't want to," Finn replied, trying to keep the whine out of her voice, knowing she sounded like a sulky child. "There's nothing to do."

"It's up to you to find things, Finn. The other two are managing, why can't you? You could make some kind of an effort."

She turned away from Finn, going back to her conversation with Jack, picking up the thread as if her daughter had not come in. They were sitting close together and there was a feeling of "two's company" about them. Finn left the house, disconcerted, shocked even. She was not used to sharing her mother's attention with anyone but her brothers.

She took the path to the beach feeling distinctly left out of everything, but she couldn't blame anyone but herself. She'd been horrible to Aidan when he'd tried to include her. She'd been horrible to both of them most of the time that they had been here. Aidan was right. She used to enjoy rock-pooling. She had spent time on other holidays beachcombing and looking for fossils. So what had changed? She had. She thought herself too old, too grown up, too sophisticated for that kind of stuff. As if all you could care about was boys and music and make-up. It was all her friends seemed to care about, but they weren't here, were they? So why did she act as if her every move was being assessed by some invisible posse?

She'd been horrible to Mike most of all. Snappish and sneering, for no good reason. He wasn't her type, and she'd thought he was trying too hard, being too nice, and that got on her nerves. Not her type? How shallow was that? And maybe he hadn't been *trying* at all. Maybe he was that kind of person: interested in everything, not just himself. She had a guilty feeling that she had badly misjudged him. He'd been genuinely pleasant and friendly ever since that first morning: to Mum, to her, to the boys. He'd been really kind to them; going out of his way to show them a good time – even if he had nearly drowned them in the process.

She was the one out of step. She felt a rush of impatience with herself. She'd go after them now, try to catch them, join the expedition. Mum was right. It was time to make an effort.

She saw them to the right of the harbour, at the far edge of the sand where spines of black rocks showed, running down to the sea in a series of seaweeded ridges, like the skeletal fingers of a long bony hand.

"Hi, I've come to join you," she yelled as soon as she came within hailing distance. "Wait for me!"

Aidan turned as he heard her.

"Great! You can hold my bucket."

He smiled as she came nearer. One good thing about Aidan, he never held grudges.

"Have you got much?" She poked about in the piled seaweed, dark and slippery as liquorice.

"We've got a few." He emptied his net, tipping out a little greenish-grey crab which dug itself down into the weed, pale legs scrabbling.

"We're going round there next," he pointed to the ridge of rocks jutting from the bulging headland. "Mike says there's some good pools and that's where the lugs are. We should be able to dig for them, that's if the tide's not too far in." Conn and Mike were already making their way around the point. They turned to beckon and Aidan waved back. "Come on," he said to Finn.

She followed, glad that she was wearing her old trainers. The rocks were slippery with clinging weed, and sharp, laid out in lines. It was like walking over a set of kitchen knives.

"Hi," Mike turned in surprise. "I thought you weren't coming."

"I changed my mind." Finn picked her way carefully towards him and Conn.

They were standing on a large rock, the last of a line tumbling down from the steeply pitched headland.

"Come up." He held out a hand. "You'll get a better view from here. This is Yellowstone Cove."

Finn looked to the top of the towering cliff. She must have been up there yesterday.

"I can't see any yellow stones." Conn looked round. "Just grey and black and brown."

"The stones are small," Mike made a space between finger and thumb. "Not much bigger than that. They aren't all yellow. Some are orange and brown. You'll find them along the shoreline or scattered over the sand. Flint, they are. Not from round here. . ."

Before Conn could ask where they came from, Aidan interrupted.

"Brilliant pools!" He swung the bucket at his side. His eyes shining at the prospect of all the crabs he was going to find.

"Yeah, great place for crabbing," Mike nodded. "You might even find some edible ones."

"What's the difference?" Conn asked.

"I'll show you, if we find some. You can take them home for your tea. Come on." He jumped down on to the hard wet sand. "We haven't got all day. We'll have to keep an eye on the time and the tide. We don't want to get cut off here."

The bay in front of them was small, a horseshoe shape cut deep into sheer over-hanging cliffs. It looked like an aquarium that had just been emptied. Water pooled deep, fringed with swaying weed, spreading out between stumpy clumps and fists of rock. Huge boulders lay singly or stacked up, dwarfing Conn and Aidan wading beneath them. Finn stayed on her rock. She wanted to call out a warning. She held her hand to her mouth, trying to stifle a sudden fear that, any moment, the whole lot could tumble down like giants' building blocks.

The sand was dark and wet right up to the cliff, not powdery like the beach by the house. This beach sloped steeply, rivered and fissured into miniature rock-strewn valleys. Her eyes flicked to the high cliff and back again. This place must fill right to the brim, then empty like a tank.

Aidan looked up from his exploring, shouting for her to come and join him. Finn shook her head and stayed where she was, shivering despite the hot sun above. She did not want her foot printed here. This was like the beach in her dreams of drowning.

"What's the matter?" Mike came back to her.

"Nothing."

"Do you need a hand getting down?"

"No, thanks."

She didn't want to be treated like some old lady and she'd had enough of him thinking she was scared of everything. Reluctantly, she jumped down, landing next to him, as light and graceful as a gymnast. She drew herself up to her full height and set out, shoulders back, matching him stride for stride, determined to hide her fear.

Chapter Eleven

Although Finn didn't want them to think that she was scared, it was not long before she suggested going back. The others would not hear of it.

"We only just *got* here!"

"Seems a shame, now we made the effort. . ."

"Don't be stupid, Finn!"

Finn gave up and began helping Aidan search the rock pools. The quicker they filled the buckets the better.

Conn and Mike were wandering along the low water mark. Mike pointed out casts and likely places, while Conn dug into the hard sand for worms. Every now and then Mike bent down to pick something up, searching under strands of weed, sorting through shells and pebbles. Soon he had a fistful.

"What are you collecting?" Finn went over, curiosity getting the better of her.

"Stones." He held out his hand. Small pebbles lay on his outstretched palm. Yellowy-orange in colour, rounded and polished by sea and sand. "They are flint, see? Very hard." He picked one out and turned it round. The surface was chipped, showing the opaque mineral interior. "Even the sea can't smooth it completely."

"What's so special?" Conn stopped his digging. The hole he had been working on immediately filled with gurgling water. "Looks like any other pebble."

"Not quite. You'll only find them on this beach. They don't occur round here naturally." Mike looked up at the cliffs. "Not part of the geology."

"So what are they doing here, then?"

"Ballast. Washed up after a wreck. Remember I told you about the wrecks? That first day when you found the bone?" Conn nodded. "Well, here's actual proof." Mike's fist closed over the stones. "These pebbles formed the ballast of a ship wrecked here: the *Anna Marie*."

"Isn't that the name of Griffiths' boat?"

Mike's eyes went as hard as the stones he clicked between his fingers.

"Yes, it is. The original *Anna Marie* foundered on the Vipers and broke up. The ballast was washed in here, along with wreckage – and bodies."

"Bodies?" He had all Conn's attention now.

"Oh, yes," Mike's eyes scanned the length of the shore and then looked back to where the cove narrowed into the cliff. "There was terrible loss of life. No one survived. The ship was bound for Bristol, carrying slaves, some say, or prisoners of war. They were held in irons below decks. When the ship hit, they stood no chance. People on the shore had seen the ship foundering and after the storm had blown over, they flocked from far and near. They found the whole cove chock-full with bodies, most of them still in their chains. There was no way of getting them up, so they buried them deep in the sand. Over there, under the cliff," he indicated behind them. "But that was not what they had come for. The ship was carrying a fortune in treasure: gold and silver, dollars, doubloons, jewels and ivory. They searched between the bodies, combing the shore, like so many birds, picking up what they could find. There was gold and silver for the taking, coins washing about in the shingle. The cove was called Dollar Cove for years after. Some people stayed so long that the tide was turning. They'd collected so much that they couldn't carry it away, so they stashed it in the caves up in the cliff. When they came back the next morning, the caves were empty. All they found was sand." He laughed. "Probably someone nicked it in the night, but some say the ship was captained by the Devil himself and he used the hours of darkness to claim his treasure back. Doesn't stop folks looking. Weekends they're up here with metal detectors and everything."

"Do they find much?" Conn asked, his eyes shining with excitement.

"Yeah, coins on the beach, now and again. As for the caves," Mike shrugged, "I don't know."

"You mean there could be treasure here?" Conn looked round. "Anywhere?"

Mike shrugged again. "Could be."

"Wow! Where would you look?"

"Along the shoreline, over the sand, but—"

Digging for worms was abandoned. Conn was running to tell Aidan.

". . .there's not much chance of it," Mike finished, but there was only Finn to hear him.

The two boys had scattered. They were soon walking, heads bent in intense concentration, stopping every now and again to sift through the weed and shingle or pick up something from the sand.

Finn rolled her eyes. "Did you *have* to tell them that? We'll never get them off here now."

"What's the matter? Don't you like it here?"

"No, I don't."

"It does have a grisly history—"

"It's not that," Finn said quickly.

"What is it then?"

Finn looked up at him, half-wondering whether to tell him that the place reminded her of a dream she kept having but, just as quickly, she dismissed the possibility.

"It's just. . ." she glanced round at the mouthed narrow cove and its lowering overhanging cliffs. "It just makes me feel uncomfortable. When the tide's in, it must fill up like a fish tank." She shuddered. "I just don't like the idea of that."

She looked up at him, expecting him to laugh, but his face was serious.

"You're right. We will have to leave before the tide turns." He looked out to where the sea was curling lazily to shore and then back to the sheer cliffs. "Or we'll be cut off." He glanced at his watch. "I'm keeping an eye on the tide, don't worry about that."

The boys found no coin, but they did find the entrance to a cave. Aidan discovered it first, and alerted Conn. They looked over to Mike and Finn, deep in conversation. Better not to tell them, especially *her*, in case they weren't allowed.

"Anyway," Conn pointed out reasonably. "If we *do* tell them, and then we find the treasure, we might have to share it."

"Yeah!" Aidan agreed, warming to the idea. "This way we get to keep it all ourselves! What do you reckon's in there?" he asked after a moment or two. "Besides treasure, I mean."

"Other stuff left by smugglers, or by wreckers. . ."

"Yeah!" Aidan nodded vigorously.

"And there could be bones," Conn's eyes lit up. "More bones, like on the other beach, but this time we can collect them. There could be a *skull*, even. Maybe we could take it home."

Aidan wrinkled his nose. "Mum wouldn't like that."

"She doesn't have to know! We can collect any finds and put them in the buckets covered with seaweed. What are we waiting for? Come on." He waved his brother towards the entrance to the cave, then he stopped. "Oh, no. I've just thought of something."

"What?"

"It's going to be dark in there. How are we going to *see* anything? I wish we'd brought a torch," he added, brow furrowing.

"Who said we didn't?" Aidan grinned and swung down his pack.

"Good old Aidie!" Conn patted him on the back. "OK, then. Let's get to it."

"I'll go and get the buckets."

When it was time to leave, her brothers were nowhere to be seen. Finn scanned the beach, and then the base of the cliff. The rock strata flowed in contorted scribbles, arching over a gap in the middle. Blue and red blobs leaned against the rock face. Buckets at the mouth of a cave.

"They'll have only gone in a little way," Mike said, glancing uneasily out to sea. The surf was building, the waves were breaking nearer. "They won't get far without a torch."

"I wouldn't put it past them to have one." Finn bit her lip, trying to control her panic. "How much time have we got?"

"Plenty," Mike lied, as he depressed two buttons on the side of his watch and read the dial. "The tide's not due in for a while." He didn't want to alarm her too much and there *was* time enough. Just. "Come on, let's get after them."

He began to run up the beach to the cave before she could ask any more. He didn't want to tell her, didn't want to freak her further but, once the tide turned, the sea came in with the speed of a train. There was no way off the beach. She'd been right about that. When the tide was in, the cove filled up like a tank.

Chapter Twelve

The narrow entrance to the cave opened out into a wide space which obviously filled at high tide. The sand inside was wet, hard-packed. Water lay in wide pools under walls studded with limpets and fringed with trailing clumps of bladderwrack. Mike called out, but got no response. There was no sign of Aidan or Conn.

The cave went back for some distance, then split into two.

"I'll take this side," Finn pointed left. "You take that."

Mike shook his head. "We better stick together."

The caves went back for ever. It was possible to get lost. They were in more danger than she knew.

"They can't have got far." He said again, as much for himself as for her. "We'll try this way first." He indicated the right hand cave.

The tunnel was wide, high-sided. Sand gave way to rock. Here and there, dark stagnant water pooled across the floor. They were soon out of sight of the entrance, reduced to feeling their way with the help of occasional flashes from a lighter Mike carried in his pocket.

"Where the hell are they?"

Mike stopped so suddenly, Finn nearly fell over him. It was cold in here. Finn shivered, clinging on to Mike's shoulder. As he leaned forward to peer into the thick darkness, the feeble flame from the lighter sputtered.

"That's not going to last much longer." He flicked it off.

"Maybe they didn't go this way."

"Maybe they didn't. We better not go any further. We ought to go back."

He turned towards her. It was so dark that she could not see his face, but she could hear his fear.

"Aidan! Conn!" She yelled, her voice echoing off the rocky walls. "Come back! Come out where we can see you!"

They both peered into the thick blackness, straining intensely. Nothing. Just water dripping. Then they both heard something. Splashing, followed by Aidan's voice.

"Finn? That you?" He sounded scared.

"Yes! Here!"

Mike felt his shoulders relax, as if a burden had fallen from them.

"They've got a torch," he said as the weak beam hit the wall.

"That'll be Aidan," Finn laughed, his relief spreading to her. "He carries everything in that pack."

"Take it easy." Mike called out, as light bobbed unevenly towards them. "Don't rush, you might trip on something."

The two boys came stumbling round a wide curving

bend, their faces white with fright in the yellow halo of the torchlight.

"Where have you been?" Finn felt like shaking them both senseless.

"It was his fault!" Aidan pointed at Conn. "We nearly got lost."

"No it wasn't!" Conn shook his head in vehement denial.

"Yes it was. You said to go further. Try one cave after another. It was your idea to look for treasure—"

"No it wasn't! It was *your* idea. *You* found the cave, *you* had the torch!"

"Never mind that now." Mike pressed a button on the side of his watch to illuminate the dial. "Give me that a minute."

He held his hand out for the torch and directed the beam down on to his wrist. Then he shook his arm and held the watch to his ear.

"What's the matter?"

"It's stopped." He squinted at the unchanging figures. "I don't believe it. You're supposed to be able to drive a truck over it. Anyone else got one?"

"I left mine at home," Finn said and the two boys shook their heads.

"Maybe it needs a new battery." Aidan suggested.

"I put one in last week. This can't happen." he shook it again. "This watch is shockproof, waterproof to a depth of two hundred feet."

"So?" Aidan shrugged. "What does it matter? Let's get out of here."

"The tide, stupid!" Mike turned on him. "It's coming in! And I have no idea how long we've been in here! Have you any concept of the trouble we're in?"

Aidan and Conn looked up at him. Until now he'd seemed the ideal big brother. A million times better than a big sister; they'd got one of those, so they ought to know. He wasn't moody like her, and he was a boy, so he was like them but better, because he was older and could do more things. But now he looked much older, his face was hard and tight, stern in the torch light. The two boys moved closer together. He looked like a man. He looked like Dad.

He stared back at them, a muscle jumping in his cheek, then he turned on his heel and led the way back towards the cave entrance. It was easier with the torch, faster going, but the stretches of water seemed wider and deeper. The surges were small, barely perceptible, but centimetre by centimetre, the pools were filling.

No one spoke as they waded on through the coldness of the water. Even the boys were silenced by the seriousness of the situation, their hearts growing heavy with deep creeping fear.

Chapter Thirteen

The cave entrance was white and frothing. Surf was boiling into the wide chamber. The water was knee deep and rising rapidly. The two bright plastic buckets were bobbing about on the surface; their creature contents spilling out to unexpected freedom, struggling through unspooling lengths of free-floating weed.

"Back!" Mike ordered. "We'll have to go back! We'll never get through that!"

"Where to?" Finn asked, but he did not answer, just turned and waded back into the cave system that they had just left. Her brothers looked to her. She shrugged. They had no other choice but to follow him.

The sound of the surf followed too, echoing through the tunnels, amplified and distorted until it became impossible to tell if it was coming from behind or in front. The water round their feet was surging much more strongly now, rising from their ankles to their knees.

"Keep together!" Mike called back. "Hold on to each other!"

They obeyed him instinctively; trusting that he alone knew what he was doing, knew the way out. Mike led on, torch in hand. He did not turn round. He did not want them to see that he had no idea where he was leading them, no idea of how to get out of here. He held the torch steady, playing it from floor to ceiling, looking for obstacles, for the walls to begin closing in on them. In its brief illumination, bulging rocks cast shadows like monsters hunched in wait and the yellow beam did not reach far. Beyond the torchlight lay a blackness as thick and impenetrable as the ocean depths.

They followed the twists and turns of the cave system, stumbling, feeling their way, unable to trust the dim light of the torch. The beam was weakening, the yellow circle getting smaller. The air around them was dank and it smelt strong and rank, like the inside of a shell.

The tunnel was narrowing; there was hardly enough room to squeeze through. The boys were moving freely enough, but Mike would soon have to work his way sideways. This looks like a dead end, Finn thought, fear grabbing her throat. They would have to go all the way back. But back to what? She had not wanted to say anything, did not want to panic the boys, but it had dawned on her some time ago that Mike did not know a way out of here. He was as much at a loss as they were.

"Mike. Wait." Finn reached forward, jogging his arm.

Mike jumped. His elbow jarred on a spur of rock and the torch spun out of his grip, falling to the floor. It lay, the light stuttering and flickering. Then it went out.

The total darkness made sight impossible, rendered everything invisible, but it left other senses enhanced.

Mike swore under his breath, each muttered curse quite audible through the creak of denim as he fumbled for his lighter again. In the following silence, the distant swell and boom of the sea grew louder, merged with the beating thud of Finn's own blood. From behind her came stereo breathing, her brothers' gulping and wheezing, each breath made shallow by terror.

Beyond that, she thought she heard something else. She put her head on one side, cocked to listen. It could be the movement of air through the passages, the trickle of water through the rocks, but she thought she heard a collective sighing, followed by a kind of low chuckling. A strange sound. Almost human. It seemed to be coming from somewhere in front of them, or was it behind? Finn felt her ears move on her head, the hairs stirring on the back of her neck.

"Did you hear that?" She whispered. "Did you hear it?"

"Hear what? Wait. I can feel something. . ." Mike said, turning, sniffing the air like a dog.

Finn inhaled sharply. Pungent ammonia and iodine, salt and seaweed, laced with a hint of something rotten.

"Ugh," she coughed. "That's horrible!"

"Not the smell. The air. It's stirring. Can't you feel it?"

"Yes," Finn put her hand to her cheek.

"It's coming from further in. Don't you see what it means?"

"No," Finn shook her head.

"It means somewhere down there is open to the air. There has to be another entrance! Come on!"

Mike took her hand and she reached back for Aidan who held on to Conn. One by one they wriggled through a narrow gap into a much larger chamber. To Finn's intense relief the smell had begun to subside and she was no longer surrounded by impenetrable blackness. The whole area was suffused by a very faint light.

Mike looked around. "There has to be a way through to the outside. A blowhole most probably. . ."

"A what?"

"A hole to the surface made by compressed air and water wearing away the overlying rock." He moved towards the strengthening source of light. "Up there, see?"

They all surged forward. The hole was not large, but it was big enough to provide an escape route out of the place. It was high above them, but the side of the cave came down in natural steps made from the scree and debris fallen from the roof. The top was just high enough for Mike to reach up and grasp the tufts of grass spilling down from the world above. He climbed on to the platform and stretched his arms, tugging on the grass.

"I think that'll just about hold. I'll go first, then Conn and Aidie you climb on Finn's shoulders, then I'll pull Finn up last."

It seemed like a good enough plan, and it all worked fine, until it came to Finn's turn.

Mike leaned right over to get her, the two younger boys hanging on to his legs. Finn stretched up as high as she could and grasped on to his hands. His grip was firm and strong, but as she reached up, the platform beneath her feet began to slide away. She was standing on a pile of splintery shards of fallen rock. The whole mass was unstable. Unable to cope with all the activity, it was beginning to subside in a mini avalanche. Finn scrabbled for more purchase, but only succeeded in making it worse. Her hands were cold and wet, she felt her fingers slipping out of Mike's. If he leaned out much further, he took the risk of falling down on top of her. He had to let go.

"Are you all right?" He called down into the chasm.

"Yes," Finn's voice came back. "I think so."

She was not hurt, just a bit shaken with a few scrapes and bruises to elbows and knees. It was a good thing that she'd been wearing jeans. She was sitting, legs sprawled, on a pile of mud and shale. She got to her feet. The circular hole in the roof was now out of reach. Her mind skittered about, trying to think of ways out. To try and climb would be dangerous. The rock broke away under her fingers and, anyway, the walls were almost sheer, rising to an impossible overhang. It looked as though she could be stuck down here, at least for a while. She sat down again, hugging her knees to stop from shaking, and tried to swallow down her fear.

"Hang on," Mike's head reappeared. "Aidie's got an idea."

"Don't worry, I'm not going anywhere," she called back, but his head had gone again. Her voice travelled away through the lengths of the caves and came echoing back, hollow and strange in the darkness. It was a lonely sound.

Chapter Fourteen

Finn kept her eyes fixed on the circle of light above her head. It was probably less than a minute since Mike's face had disappeared, but it felt like longer. Alone down here, time seemed to stretch.

The hole in the roof was almost perfectly round; tufts of grass hung down like fringing hair. Finn stood up to ease her stiffness and rubbed her arms. Seeing the sky and sun reminded her that it was cold down here. And getting colder. Then there was the smell.

Finn's nostrils twitched and flared. The rotten fishy stench that she had detected earlier was there again and getting stronger. Maybe it was the movement of the sea through the caves, compressing the air, pushing it towards her. . .

She jerked her head. There was a sound. Faint at first, a kind of rushing whisper, like water under pressure, but getting louder, turning into a chuckling chatter, like stones clacking together. It must be the tide washing through the tunnels. . .

Finn looked around, trying to locate the direction of the sound. The way to the sea lay to the right, that was the way they had come, she was pretty sure, but the sounds were not coming from that direction. They were coming from the left, which meant they were coming from deeper in, where the cave twisted away under the land.

The noises coming towards her were not being made by surf or water. The smell was growing more intense, building until the cave seemed filled with the gagging distillation of every kind of fishy rottenness. Finn masked her nose and mouth with her arm to stop herself from retching. Fear and nausea swept over her in waves, threatening to overwhelm her. She could not tell what was beyond the corner, but her senses told her that it was a thing of indescribable horror.

"Quick! Mike! Anyone up there! You've got to help me!"

She tried to yell, but terror closed her throat and all that came out was a strangled squeak. She directed her voice up towards the circle of sky above, but her words seemed to fall back from there and get swallowed by the darkness. The other sound seemed nearer, spreading out around her, shifting from clacking chatter to something deeper, like boulders tumbled together, or rumbling laughter. Behind it came the whisper of water and she could hear her name being repeated over and over. It was as if the sea itself was calling for her.

She could still see nothing. She licked her lips, her mouth dried by fear, and flattened herself against the rock wall, facing out into the cave, holding her eyes wide, moving her head from side to side. Still nothing.

Then she saw it. The tiniest of movements, a flash of white in a background dense as night. It could be the glint of an eye, or the gleam of bone, or skin.

"Finn?" The voice from above jolted through her like an electric shock. "Here, grab on to this."

Mike was leaning over, dangling something into the gap. Finn recognized the broad yellow straps of Aidan's rucksack. She leapt up, grasping hold of the webbing, one foot kicking for the side of the cave. She was almost there, almost free, then she felt something fasten round her other ankle. Something intent on dragging her back. Something cold and clammy. She looked down, almost expecting to see her foot tangled in seaweed. That's what it felt like, but nothing grew down here. . .

"What's the matter?" Mike called.

"I've got my foot caught. . ."

"What is it, Finn? What is it?"

There was no reply, but he could feel that there was suddenly something badly wrong. Finn was struggling, the bag twisting in his hands. It was almost as much as he could do to hold her.

"You two grab hold of the side pockets," He yelled to Conn and Aidan. "Pull on the count of three. One, two, three! Again. One, two. . ."

Together they hauled, like a team in a tug of war. Finn had stopped struggling now. She held on from pure instinct. She had looked down, still thinking to see her ankle wrapped by weed or something, but instead she had seen a hand. The thin curling fingers were white and livid, almost luminous in the darkness, the back was marked with a dull bluish pattern, like a web or an open-weave glove. The grasp was strong, and as cold as clay. The hand of a dead man held her fast.

Chapter Fifteen

"It's all right. It's all right. I've got you."

Shaking and sobbing, Finn clung to Mike, tears streaming down her face. Her brothers stared in round-eyed wonder, they had rarely seen her in this kind of state. She didn't care. She just wanted someone to hold her.

"Hey, hey, you're soaking my shirt." Mike waited for the crying to subside, before prising her gently from his chest. He pushed her hair back and looked into her eyes. "How you feeling? Better?"

Finn nodded, sobs reduced to the occasional shudder.

"Good." He smiled and held her for another moment before letting her go. "Anything useful in that pile of junk?" He indicated the contents of Aidan's rucksack strewn across the clifftop. "Like a drink or something? While you're looking, hand us that towel."

Aidan gave the towel for Finn to wipe her face, then rummaged about and came up with a bottle of mineral water.

"Sit down for a bit. Take a drink. It'll make you feel better."

Finn did as she was told. Gradually the horror

receded enough for her to take in her surroundings. They were above Yellowstone Cove, not very far from where she was yesterday, but a long way back from the cliff-face.

"What happened down there?" Mike asked after a while.

Finn looked down at her ankle. In her mind she could see the hand again, the fingers wrapping round it. She shook her head. She must have imagined it, fear making her hallucinate.

"I don't know," she said. "Just got spooked, I guess."

"Pack that stuff up." Mike turned to Aidan. "We better be getting back."

He automatically checked his watch. The LCD remained frozen. Conn nudged him and he looked up. There was a man coming along the cliff path. It looked like Griffiths.

"Where did he spring from?"

"Over on that headland." Conn nodded towards the point where the land fell away to the sea. "He was standing there a while."

Griffiths passed close enough for them to see his sardonic grin. His dark eyes gleamed amusement at their dishevelled state and his raised black eyebrows seemed to be asking if they were having a nice time. Mike pointedly looked away and ignored him, but when he glanced at his watch, the LCD had changed. It was working again, almost from the exact time that Griffiths walked by them. Funny that.

*

Finn woke covered in sweat. This was the worst dream since she had been here; quite possibly the worst dream ever. It started, as it always did, with the distant crash and grind of surf on pebbles. A twist of the lens of the mind served to make memory and dream combine, so this was no longer just *the beach*, it was Yellowstone Cove. Sweat broke out anew as Finn reviewed the events of the dream. Usually she woke when the waves crashed over her. Not this time.

She had been out of herself, looking down at her body as though it belonged to someone else, seeing it twisting and spinning, rolled by the vicious undertow. She saw her hair, like bright thin strands of red-gold weed, scarfed across her blue-lipped, blind-eyed face. She was wearing the green swimsuit, the one with the white straps and stripes down the side. She looked like one already dead. Helpless to resist the rotating flow of the waves' surge, she was answering the call, letting herself be hauled back and back to quieter, deeper water, away from the roaring shore.

She sat up in bed, arms folded. She would sit up all night if necessary, rather than be sucked back into that dream again. The wind had got up since yesterday afternoon. It was howling round the house now. On the roof the plastic sheeting flapped and snapped. Somewhere a door or window banged. Finn found the noise comforting rather that disconcerting. At least it was real.

Finn must have dozed off despite her intentions. The

wind woke her. It was gusting, building to a crescendo, then leaving a lull. That was when she heard it. In that little pocket of silence. Creaking. The sound of weight bearing down on wood, a deliberate, stealthy movement and it was coming from outside her window. She must be dreaming. Not awake after all. It was happening again. Just like before. Her curtains partially open. The sky showing blackness. A quick burst, a kind of patter. First one, then another. A spatter of something hitting the glass. . .

Finn sat up, realizing that the window was open. She got out of bed, stumbling across the room to close it, although it had been shut before, she was certain of it.

There is someone outside. She sees one figure, then another. It's not Aidan out there, or Conn. This is something quite other. Shadowy figures, insectlike in their skeletal thinness, scaling the scaffolding like rigging, swarming up it with horrible agility.

Finn is unable to move. Terror is spreading through her, immobilizing her like some swift-acting drug. There's a hand on the window. Fingers spread wide. White against the blackness, it looks like the underside of a starfish. As she stares, the hand slides down, creeping in to grasp the sill. If she looks down, she will see the strange marking etched across the back. The mark shows black. A clearly defined mapping of lines against transparent bluish skin. They make a star shape, extending from the thickened first knuckle of the middle finger down to the wrist.

She does not look down. She has cheated them once

today. She drags her eyes away and reaches up. Her arms feel dreadfully heavy and will only move slowly, but she gropes for the top of the sash, gripping it firmly and bringing the window down with a crash.

The bottom edge seems to slice through the forearm, severing the hand clean from the body. Finn reels back, shuddering, but when she looks again all she sees is water pooling, forming into transparent globules on the white paint of the ledge.

She gets back into bed, thinking all the while that this is a dream. She lies rigid, then gradually her body relaxes and she is claimed by sleep.

In the morning, Finn knew that she'd been dreaming. She woke with the thick taste in her mouth and the familiar sick headache. Gradually, remnants of the dream came back, drifting into her consciousness. She got up and went over to the window. Water still pooled on the sill. She dipped her finger and tasted salt water.

Chapter Sixteen

Mum and the boys were heading for the beach. Maggie suggested that Finn come with them, a walk by the shore might cure her headache, but Finn did not want to go anywhere near the sea. She took the road in the opposite direction, up to the village.

The village was very small. Just a little, squat-towered, grey stone church standing slightly apart from a pub, *The Smugglers' Rest*, a couple of houses and a shop ranged round a ragged patch of green.

The shop-cum-post-office sold newspapers, magazines and the usual array of sweets and snacks. A few shelves held basic provisions for visitors holidaying in the area and locals caught short after the weekly supermarket shop. The door stood open. The women at the counter went quiet when Finn walked in.

"Can I help you, love?" The plump woman standing at the till looked in her direction.

"No. I'm just looking," Finn answered, but the woman's attention was already turning back to her other customers. They didn't seem to be buying anything. Their accents placed them as locals, in for a gossip.

Finn felt awkward, an intruder. She made a pretence

of browsing for a while and then left. On her way out she managed to collide with a stand full of beach toys. Fishing nets scattered like toothpicks; Styrofoam body-boards knocked over a pile of plastic buckets sending them rolling all over the pavement. The women by the counter turned to stare. Finn flushed deep pink and scurried to pick them all up.

"I'd have thought you'd have had enough of those yesterday. Here, let me." Mike bent to help her. "How are you feeling? OK?"

"I'm fine. What are you doing here?" she asked, as he re-stacked the stand.

"Sent up to get snap for the boys." He nodded towards the counter and the fridge next to it. "They depend on a regular supply of drinks, fags and snacks. Can't work without it."

The woman smiled as he gave his order. They talked and laughed together, exchanging quick words in Welsh. Her whole face and manner relaxed as she chatted, changing from the casual indifference Finn had experienced into something much more animated. Mike was clearly quite a favourite.

"This is Finn," he said by way of introduction.

"Hello, love. I'm Nerys." The woman extended a plump hand. "I run the *Smuggler's* and this place."

"She's staying at the Salt House."

"Ah, your mum's been up a couple of times. I did wonder. Seen you about, like."

Nerys continued to smile at her, but the other women at the counter looked at each other.

"Your mum the one that bought it?"

Finn shook her head. "My aunt."

"On holiday, then?"

Finn nodded.

"That's nice. How are you finding it?"

"OK. Fine."

"Nice restful time?"

"Um, yes, I guess. . ."

"Nice. That's nice." Nerys gave her another smile, then added something in Welsh to Mike as she handed over his order.

He nodded and smiled, replying in the same language, calling back, "See you, Nerys," as he headed for the door.

She added another comment, again in Welsh, but Mike just laughed and gave her a wave.

"What did she say?" Finn asked when they left the shop.

"Nothing." Mike shrugged but Finn knew he was lying by the way he was colouring up.

"Are you sure?"

"Course."

"She must have said something."

"It was nothing."

"How many words do you need to say nothing? Tell me."

"OK," his colour deepened. "She said you were very pretty."

"Oh," Finn had not been expecting that.

"Don't get them wrong." Mike sensed her thoughts.

"They aren't unfriendly. More like shy, really. She doesn't know you, see? Known me since I was this high." He indicated somewhere round his knee. "We used to live here when I was little."

"Why did you move?"

"Dad wanted to be in town. Nearer the port, for his work."

"What does he do?" Finn was curious. She realized she knew almost nothing about him, his family, his home life.

"He's a pilot."

Finn frowned, as if what he was saying didn't add up.

"Not the flying kind," Mike laughed. "He brings ships in, tankers and that, into the refinery, and ferries into the terminal."

"Does your mum work?"

"Part-time in a dentist's surgery. The rest of the time she looks after my little brother."

"I didn't even know you *had* a little brother." She should have guessed, though. That's why he was so good with Conn and Aidan.

"Oh, yes. George."

"How old is he?"

"Seven. A couple of years younger than Conn. He was a bit of an afterthought. I don't think Mam was expecting any more. I've got an older sister. She's away at the moment, working abroad."

"Oh, right." Finn fell silent. Suddenly his life was full of people she hadn't even guessed at. It had not even occurred to her to ask before.

"What's that?"

They were passing the churchyard. Finn pointed to a tall Celtic cross standing just inside the entrance.

"It marks a mass grave." He held the small wooden gate open for her. "The *Nancy Drew*, lost with all hands. It was an emigrant ship, heading for Canada when it struck the Vipers on May the third, 1855. It went down, all hands. 193 men, women and children, all drowned." He turned and pointed to a smaller monument, a plain slate stone shaded by a tree. "That's there for the lifeboat crew who tried to go to their rescue."

Finn went over and read the inscription:

To the glory of God and in memory of those men who lost their lives in coming to the rescue of. . .

She read down the list of names. Goosebumps prickled her flesh. Two were surnamed Treherne.

"There are lots of us buried here," Mike said quietly.

Finn looked around, registering the names on different headstones. Some were old, lichen-covered, inscriptions worn away and hard to see. Others looked much more recent, the carving clear, standing out in sharp relief. Many had lived out their three score and ten, but a number were marked as drowned, or perished with those they sought to save. Their names were listed among those lost in a number of disasters: John, William, George Treherne. Pilot.

"Dangerous thing to be, ships' pilot," Mike remarked as he pointed the names out to her. "Now here's an interesting one." He pointed to a small stone, chunky

118

and squat, scrolled across the top and marked with an equal-sided cross. "They call him The Devil's Pilot."

"Was he drowned, too?" Finn knelt down, parting the grass to find the date. "Can't have been," she quickly calculated in her head. "He'd have been too old. . ."

"No. He lived to tell the tale."

"Why do they call him the Devil's Pilot?"

"He went out to the *Anna Marie*. You know, the ship wrecked in Yellowstone Cove, where we were yesterday? The one I was telling you about?"

"Why do they call him the Devil's Pilot?"

"One dark and stormy night, they heard a gun go off. A distress signal. A ship in trouble. Sure enough, off St Mary's Head a frigate is spotted. She must have been trying to make the Haven, but there's a strong nor'westerly and a heavy sea. She's on the wrong course altogether, either blown there, or lured away, because she's off the main channel, heading in towards the Vipers and Westwater Bay." Mike's eyes grew distant as if he could see it all happening before him. "That ship proved to be the *Anna Marie*. John Treherne goes out to help her. As pilot it's his job to render assistance, but when he gets there, the captain turns him back. He's standing at the rail, a tall man, black-bearded, and dressed all in black. 'Pilot away!' he shouts over the side, the wind snatching the words from his mouth. 'We are beyond assistance here. Save yourself! I'll not have *your* death on my conscience. We are bound for hell.'

"False lights showed up on the cliff. The *Anna Marie* had been lured to her fate. The pilot and his crew were already too late. The ship was doomed. It had struck the Vipers. As it began to break up, sailors threw themselves from the rigging into the raging sea and from below decks came such a moaning and shrieking, it seemed to the pilot and his men that the ship was full of souls already in torment. They did what they could, but no one was saved." Mike shook his head dolefully. "But that's not the end of the story. . ." He dropped his voice, making it low and spooky.

"Well, go on," Finn urged. "What else?"

"They do say that on stormy nights a black ship, square-rigged, comes into the bay with all sails set, moving against the wind and the run of the tide, and not a soul to be seen aboard her. They say it's the Devil's own ship and that he's come back to haunt those who lured him on to the rocks. . . Hey!" Mike exclaimed as the colour drained from Finn's face. "It's just a story!" He dipped his head to see into her eyes. "I didn't scare you, did I?"

"Of course not!" Finn turned away, not wanting him to see how shaken she was. "I'm not a little kid. That story wouldn't even scare Conn and Aidie."

But it scared *you*, all right, Mike thought. He wanted to ask why, but judged that now was probably not the best time. He was beginning to really like Finn. He'd been glad to see her up at the shop. He wanted to know her better, despite her unpredictable mood swings and gimlet-sharp remarks. Yesterday, she'd seemed to mellow – a bit anyway. He had even thought to ask her out on a date or something. She was scowling at him now, a frown furrowing her brow. Maybe not just yet.

"Sorry," he held up his hands. "Whatever I've done. I didn't mean. . ."

"It's OK," Finn sighed. "It's nothing to do with you. I didn't sleep very well last night, that's all."

They walked on in silence. Finn seemed pre-occupied, almost as if she'd forgotten he was there. Mike looked around, searching for something to interest her.

"Here's a good one."

Mike pointed to another headstone. It was old-looking, leaning forward slightly, the worn inscription fast disappearing under a lacy covering of grey and yellow lichen.

"He's the reason we're here."

"What do you mean?"

"*Treherne* isn't a local name. It's Cornish."

Finn bent down. She could make out the name, *James Treherne, Departed this world 1719.*

"Why is there only one date?" She asked, looking up at Mike.

"That was the date he died. No one knew when he was born."

"Why not? That seems odd."

"He was washed up in a shipwreck. His mother and father were among the dead. Bodies stripped: clothes, rings, everything. It is said that the woman was still alive, but when she struggled, trying to protect her child, they killed her with one of the little hatchets they carried. His father, too, was killed for the silver buckles on his shoes. They left the lad till last, not thinking he carried anything valuable. They were stripping his clothes, prepared to leave him for dead, when one of the fishermen stepped in. Not *everyone* agreed with wrecking. It was too late to do anything for the parents, but he saw that there was life in the little lad. He took him for his own. They found his name stitched into his clothes: James Treherne."

"Who's that?"

Finn parted the grass round a small lozenge-shaped black marble stone. It was positioned near to James Treherne, but this was much newer. Recent, in fact. The cuts in the highly polished surface were sharply chiselled and fresh. Finn looked at the dates and calculated. William Treherne had died four years ago at the age of twenty-six.

"It's a marker for my uncle." Mike's voice was level and his eyes met hers, challenging her to say anything clever.

"I'm sorry." Finn apologized. The death had not been long ago. The memory was clearly still painful, not anaesthetized by time like the others. "You don't have to tell me if you don't want to. It's just," she hesitated, "he was so young."

"Yes. Tragic." It was Mike's turn to be clipped and off-hand.

"Like I said, if you don't want to talk about it. . ."

"It – it's not that. Sorry. It – it just kind of upsets me. You know?"

Finn nodded.

"It was a diving accident," Mike went on after a while. "His body was never found. That's why the stone is so small."

"What happened? How did they know? Know he was. . ."

"Dead? They took a pretty good guess. He was out on his own. . ." Mike bit his lip and frowned. "Something must have happened. They found some of his gear. Air tanks crumpled like coke cans. Wetsuit shredded to rubber bands. . ."

Mike paused, as if he did not trust himself to speak. When he went on, he was more serious than Finn had ever seen him before. His voice was laced with a practised bitterness, well-rehearsed and deeply felt. She did not feel that he was just speaking for himself.

"He shouldn't have been on his own." he said. "You're supposed to dive with a buddy, a companion, in case things go bad on you. It was supposed to be a good day for it. Weather fair, sea calm, but he was diving in Westwater Bay and out there, anything can happen. A squall can come up from nowhere – you saw the other day. Faulty gear, rip tides and currents. Diving's a dangerous business."

"What was he doing?"

"Exploring a wreck. The *Anna Marie*."

"Hang on, I thought—"

"Griffiths found it? Absolutely not." Mike's upper lip curled in a sneer. "He just took all the glory and made all the money. Will *found* it. He'd heard all the stories right from when he was a little kid. He knew it must be out there somewhere. He did lots of research: studied maps, charts, eyewitness accounts. He went to London, to search the Admiralty records. Worked abroad on short contracts to finance the first diving season. He found some cannon and an anchor that could have been from her, and then he found something else." Mike's eyes gleamed with excitement, as though he was there himself. "The water was very cold, and there was a strong current. Will was fighting to stay in one place, and the struggle let water into his mask. He tilted his head to clear it and as his vision cleared, he saw something glittering in a fissure between the rocks. He probed the crack and came out with a gold coin. Then he saw another, then another, until he had four altogether. His air had nearly run out by this time, so he made a near-free ascent back to the RIB—"

"What's an RIB?"

"Rubber inflatable boat, sorry." Mike had got so caught up in his tale he had reverted to diver-speak. "Anyway, up he went, clutching the coins so hard the imprint was on his hand for hours. Of course, word got around. That's when Griffiths got interested. He wanted to come in with Will, offered to put up money. Salvage – that's his business. But Will wasn't having any."

"Wait. Hang on a minute. I thought all the gold and stuff got washed up on the shore?"

Mike shook his head. "Not all. The ship contained the

captain's personal treasure. Some said he had been a pirate, a buccaneer; he was a bit of a mystery figure, but very wealthy, by all accounts. What was washed up would have been only a fraction of what was on board. And it was all there, Will reckoned, trapped in this gully he'd found."

"So what happened?"

"Will should have reported the find straight away, to the Receiver of Wrecks – that's who you have to tell – but he didn't. He wanted to verify what he'd found first. That was his mistake. Not long after that first dive, he had his accident. After that, Griffiths took over, reported the wreck as *his* discovery."

"He couldn't do that, surely?"

"Why not? Will wasn't around to argue his claim, was he?"

"What about the people here? The people in the village? They must have known your uncle found it?"

"Yes, but *Griffiths* registered the find with the Receiver of Wrecks. It was in his name, and he made absolutely sure that it was all above board. Everything was done by the book. There was nothing *they* could do about it. There was talk, but Griffiths is used to that – he never has been Mr Popularity. His whole family come to that. They've always had a bad reputation."

"They were the magicians?" Finn asked, remembering her mum's conversation with Uncle Jack. "The ones who could call up storms?"

Mike nodded.

"Do people still believe in that now?" She thought about that day on the cliff, how Griffiths was there when the wind sprang up. "You know, that he could have some kind of power?"

"Not that they'd admit. But you won't find many that would go up against him. My uncle did." Mike went down on one knee and touched the shiny black stone, forefinger tracing the deeply chiselled lettering. "And look what happened to him. None of them would *work* with him – Uncle Jack saw to that – but so what?" Mike stood up and shrugged, palms out, gesturing helplessness. "He just got divers in from other places. The wreck turned out more valuable than anyone expected. Griffiths made a fortune." He folded his arms and gave a humourless laugh. "Enough to buy the cruiser and build that hideous bungalow."

"But you don't mean," Finn frowned. "You don't mean Griffiths was *involved* in some way – in your uncle's death. . ."

Mike shrugged again – who knows – his face tight and closed.

"But wouldn't they – the authorities – wouldn't they know?"

"How? With no body found? Anyway, Griffiths was miles away at the time. Loads can witness to it. Still think it was him, though." Mike muttered.

"Why?"

"He had the motive. Wanted to take the wreck for himself. He was *really* pissed off when Will wouldn't take him in on it."

"But how? How could he do it?"

"Interfere with his gear, the boat. There are lots of ways. . ."

Mike's voice tailed off. He had been told to keep his mouth shut before. He had absolutely no proof for the accusations he was making and his words were slanderous.

"But I don't care. I know he did it," he added quietly, almost to himself.

"But how do you know?"

"I feel it." He touched his chest. "I feel it in here and one day I'm going to prove it. Come on." He took her arm. "Let's get out of here. I'm beginning to find this place depressing."

Finn looked down at the small block of polished stone. Not much to show for a life.

Chapter Seventeen

"I was going to take your brothers into town this afternoon, get some fishing gear. . ." Mike said as they got near to the house. "Would you like to come?"

"I don't like fishing."

"That's not all there is. There are other shops besides the chandler's – that's where we're going for the fishing stuff – they're doing up the whole dockside area. There's cafes, and a little museum, and—"

"OK, I'll come."

"*You*'d probably think it's boring, but—"

"I said 'yes', I'd like to." Finn put her hand on his arm to stop him going on.

"Right, then," he grinned, relieved that she had agreed. "It's a date. I think you'll like the chandler's shop. It belongs to Uncle Jack. It's part of the boatyard. When I was a kid, I'd be down there every chance I got. I loved the yard, it smelt of wood and paint and varnish and I'd collect offcuts to make my own little boats. If I got bored with that, I could go into the shop. It was like stepping into heaven: packed full of surfboards, yachting stuff and fishing tackle. My Uncle Will used to run it—"

"What was he like?"

"He was the youngest. Dad and Jack were much older than him, so he never seemed like an uncle to me, more a big brother. I worshipped him. He seemed so exciting, you know? Glamorous. He was away a lot, and when he came back, he always had something for me. You know when people bring you stuff and it's never what you want? He always knew the right thing. Aussie surfing gear, when you couldn't get it here. Fake designer stuff. He bought a Rolex one time. And this."

Round his neck, Mike wore a pendant hanging from a thin black leather thong. Finn had noticed it before. He reached inside his T-shirt now, fishing it out for her to see. A little dancing man carved from what looked like dark green jade, a tongue protruding from his grimacing mouth.

"What is it?"

"A New Zealand Tiki. Maori good luck charm. He went there to surf and brought it back for me. He was a brilliant surfer. One of the really greats. When they were about my age, him and one of his mates went off round the world. Following the wave. They went everywhere: South Africa, Australia, New Zealand, Bali, Hawaii and the States, all the way up the Pacific Coast, from Mexico to Alaska. They surfed as the waves froze on the beach." He smiled, blue eyes distant. "He did the kind of things other people only dream of. I wouldn't mind doing that. Taking a gap year, just taking off. . ."

"Hmm, maybe. I don't think it would suit me." Finn

couldn't see the attraction herself. "He spent a lot of time abroad, then?"

Mike nodded. "He worked as a diver: rigs, salvage, instructor. He'd work for six months, earning good money, then he'd have six months off to do what he wanted. Not a bad way to be."

"So why did he come back here?"

"He said he was tired of wandering. Wanted to settle down. He ran the chandler's for Uncle Jack while he researched the *Anna Marie*. He was going to set up a diving school on the proceeds from that. He had lots of plans, but. . ."

Mike shrugged, palms out. The gesture spoke for itself. His uncle never had time to do what he planned. His life had ended.

They couldn't all get in Mike's pick-up, so Jack loaned him the transit. When they got to town, the chandler's was shut for lunch, the guy who ran it was probably still in the pub, so they went to the museum instead.

Once inside the main entrance, arrows directed them into a special exhibition:

The Treacherous Shore:
A History of Wreckers and Wrecking

The inside was dark. It took a minute or two for their eyes to adjust.

"Look." Conn pressed a button on a panel by his

side and lots of little bulbs lit up. "It shows where the wrecks were all along the coast."

"Wow! I never realized that there were that many! There's loads in our bay." Aidan leaned forward, to study the map. "Some of these are quite recent." He frowned. He'd always thought of wrecks as olden days stuff.

"Radar and modern navigation aids don't make the sea any less dangerous," Mike said. "It's small ships mostly, nowadays, yachts and fishing vessels, but there was a ferry grounded a couple of years ago, not to mention oil tankers getting into trouble. The Haven is one of the deepest harbours in Europe, but the entrance is narrow, not easy to negotiate in a Force Ten." He grinned. "That's where my dad comes in."

"Is that what he does, then?" Aidan was impressed.

"Yeah. He's a pilot."

"What does a pilot *do*, exactly?" Conn asked.

"He's a specialist, you have to have a license for it. He conducts ships in and out of port."

"What? Even big huge ones? Tankers and that?" Conn looked up at Mike who nodded.

"That's cool!" Aidan whistled. Mike's smile widened. He was proud of his father's job.

They all moved on to the next exhibit. A large tableau. It came to life at the touch of a button, complete with sound effects. A ship loomed out of the darkness, side on and listing horribly, its four masts and spider's web of rigging silhouetted against a painted background of mountainous seas. The moon silvered the sky behind dark ragged clouds. Different coloured lights, playing in sequence, gave an illusion of movement. Thunder cracked, each clap timed to a ripping lightning flash. The wind screamed and the waves crashed and, weaving through it all, waxing and waning on the wind, came a confusion of human voices. Desperate shouts of command mingled with anguished prayers and cries for help.

The next tableau showed the same ship in the sickly light of morning. It was nearer to shore now; the masts were down, trailing in the boiling water, tangled in a mass of rope and sail. Great timbers thrust up, jagged and splintered, as the ship lay broken like a children's toy on a wicked line of jagged rocks. On the beach a dark mass of people stood watching the ship's final death throes, spread along a foreshore already strewn with wreckage, clotted with bodies.

The crash of the surf, the grinding drag of boulder and stone were almost too much for Finn to bear. Her dreams were coming back to her. Her mouth filled with the saline taste of salt water and blood. The heavy boom of the sea was woven with other sounds, howling and crying, the screams of the dying. It seemed to her as though the whole scene was moving. The people spreading out to search and plunder, seething like maggots over carrion. They had brought carts with them, donkeys laden with panniers to haul the loot away. She wanted to reach out and stop them. She turned away with a shudder, afraid that if she did, the diminutive figures would squidge and ooze out between her fingers in a sticky mess of flesh and blood.

"Are you all right?" Mike asked, putting a hand out to steady her. "You've gone very white."

"Yes," Finn cleared her throat and nodded. "It's just very . . . life-like."

The tableau faded into darkness. Conn reached to press the button again.

"I'd rather you didn't." Finn put her hand over his. "Let's move on to the next bit."

Conn looked at his brother, eyebrows raised. Finn could be strange sometimes. Aidan shrugged.

"Might as well," he said. "I don't suppose it will do anything else."

Large glass cabinets displayed the rest of the exhibition: notices of wreck sales, lists of ships lost, artefacts recovered. Everyday objects: pots, pans, plates and tankards; some barnacle-encrusted, others as clean as the day that they went down. Personal possessions, combs, dice, thimbles, items of jewellery, lay with a scattering of gold and silver coins.

Mike stood for a while, head bowed, staring at the caption card.

Some of these exhibits were recovered from wrecks in this area. The museum would particularly like to thank Mr A Griffiths and Salvage International for kindly lending finds from the Anna Marie.

"Should have been Will," Mike muttered. "Should have been his name on that card."

They moved on to the next exhibit: *Gwyr y Bwelli Bach, the Men of the Little Hatchets.*

"Look," Aidan pointed, "There's one of the little

chopper things they cut off people's hands with." He leaned closer, lip curling in disappointment. "It's not a real one, though. Just a replica."

"That was probably donated by Griffiths and all," Mike said quietly, the bitterness still apparent in his voice. "He hasn't changed much."

"He's got one in his house," Conn said.

"Oh yeah?" Aidan sneered. "How do you know?" He shook his head. "You are *such* a blagger!"

"I'm not! I saw it."

"When?"

"When I was up at his house. . ."

"When were you up at his house?" Finn asked casually.

"When – when I was looking for my ball. I saw the hatchet thing in – in a glass cabinet." Conn finished warily, his eyes sliding away from Finn.

"Oh, yes? And how did you get to see inside this glass cabinet?"

"From – from the window."

"From the window? I don't think so."

"I did! Honest!"

"I don't believe you."

"You broke in?" Aidan's eyes widened in wonder.

"I didn't! I – I. . ." Conn looked up at his sister. She knew he was lying. "OK. What if I did?" He said finally, lower lip stuck out, brows lowered. "He shouldn't have left a window open."

"That's breaking and entering!" Finn said sternly. "Mum'd go crazy!"

"So?" He stared up at his sister, brown eyes defiant. "I was only looking. I didn't *take* anything. He stole off me, anyway. He stole my ball!"

"That's not the point! The point is—"

"What does it matter?" Mike interrupted. "He didn't get caught, did he?" He looked down at Conn. "What else did you see?"

"Nothing. Just maps and stuff on a big table, and a big telescope, and what looked like a radar screen and a short-wave radio type thing, and a computer. . ."

"You *knew* he'd been up there?" Finn turned to Mike.

"I didn't know he'd been *in*." He winked at Conn and grinned. "That took guts. Was there other stuff in this cabinet?"

"Oh, yes," Conn nodded. "A kind of collection of things but they were odd."

"How do you mean? Odd?"

"They didn't seem to go with the other stuff." Conn closed his eyes, trying to remember, like one of those games at parties – name everything on the tray. "On one shelf there was the hatchet, like that one; and a mirror but that was kind of old and battered, not very shiny at all. Next to it was a brass thing on a piece of string. Quite big and heavy looking. Tear shaped. A what-d-ya-call-it? Pendulum. That was on that shelf. The others held what looked just like bits and bobs. I didn't pay much attention, but they were pretty much like that stuff over there." He indicated the display cabinet behind them. "Oh, there was something else I forgot to mention. In one corner of the room there was a head of a lady. I thought she was real at first, then I saw she was carved out of wood." Conn grinned ruefully. "She gave me quite a shock."

"That'll be the figurehead from the *Anna Marie*." Mike looked around the museum, at the displays of finds that should have been attributed to his uncle. "He must have kept it, like his own personal trophy. Come on," he said. "I've had enough of this place."

Chapter Eighteen

They walked out on to the quay. The day was still fine, but the sun was obscured by a veil of high cloud and the boats were creaking in their berths, shifting in an increasing swell. Mike predicted a change in the weather.

"There's going to be a storm."

"How do you know?"

"Did you see the moon last night?"

Finn shook her head, "Can't say I did."

"It was new," his fingers described a thin crescent. "But you could still see the old moon with the new moon wrapped round it." His hands now made the shape of a full circle. "That's a sign. A sign of storms."

Finn looked doubtful. "It all looks pretty calm to me."

Mike shrugged. "Maybe. Lots of sailors swear by signs like that. Much more reliable than the Met office, that's what they reckon."

"How can they be?" Finn objected. "They've got satellites and everything."

"So? Didn't help them predict that hurricane did it?"

"Suppose not." Finn replied, willing to concede. After all, what did she know about the weather?

Danford Haven was a big working port and, as they went round the harbour, Mike pointed out all the different types of craft. The boys were entranced. They were interested in everything from the collection of historic ships moored along the quay outside the museum: tall sailing ships and rusting motor torpedo boats; to the car ferries as tall as buildings, entering and leaving the terminal in the outer harbour. Further out, beyond them, oil tankers lay at anchor, as big as city blocks.

"What are those?" Conn asked, pointing to a couple of short thick boats.

"Tugs. Not the prettiest, but very powerful. Heavyweights, by the look of them. Ocean going. They are used to get ships in and out of port or help them if they get into trouble." Mike squinted at the logo on the side. *IS. International Salvage*. "They belong to your friend Griffiths. His company, that is. He might look like a tramp," Mike replied to Conn's sceptical look, "but he's worth plenty. That's my dad's boat." He pointed to another powerful looking boat with PILOT on the side and front. "Well, not his personally."

"Can we go on?" Conn asked, eyes wide and pleading.

"Not now," Mike grinned, "they're working. Anyway, I thought you wanted to go to the chandler's. We're nearly there."

"I do, but. . ." Conn looked longingly at the chunky powerful craft bristling with radar and aerials.

"My dad's not there at the moment. He's not on duty until this evening. Maybe some other time. How'd that do?"

Conn nodded, eyes shining. Finn had to smile. She had never seen such a clear case of hero-worship in her life.

Finn followed them into the chandler's, prepared to be bored, but as soon as she stepped through the door on to the polished wooden floor she was enthralled.

The shop was a proper ships' chandler, catering for everyone, from the weekend sailor to the round the world yachtsman. Beautifully machined brass and stainless steel gear lay stacked next to drums of clean new rope, holding every size from thin cord to fat plaited strands thicker than a man's arm. Huge sea rods lay in racks along one wall, while another held shelves of sailing clothes and soft rubber wetsuits hanging like empty skins.

There were other things, too. Things that did not look as though they were for sale. A large polished bell and a gleaming brass lantern hung from the roof beams. A thickly ribbed, giant conch shell carried a stock of children's beach toys. An amphora stood by the far counter, pointed end held in an iron frame, white worm casts encrusting the dusty terracotta.

The shop was Conn heaven. She watched her brothers, standing together, eyes wide with wonder, taking everything in. They were drawn first to the surfers' corner and stood admiring the boards and drooling over the clothes. They looked beseechingly at Finn who shook her head. They had been given money by Mum, but it didn't run to that kind of expense. Next they went to the fishing-tackle counter and leaned on the glass, heads together, sorting through silver spinners and packets of bright feather lures while Mike talked kinds of bait, hook size and line weights with the man behind the counter.

Finn had no interest in this. As far as she was concerned, planning different ways to murder fish was strictly a boys' thing. She was staring over her brothers' heads, waiting for them to make their selection, when her attention was caught by a creased and dog-eared picture on the wall. It was in the middle of a batch of yellowing clippings: local heroes riding monster waves and making record catches. She went closer, leaning over the counter to get a better look. She'd thought it was cut from a magazine, but now she could see that it was a photograph, taken abroad in a sun strong enough to threaten overexposure.

Time had faded the print still further, distorting the colours. A man stood under a colourless sky on the deck of a white-painted vessel which floated on a pale green sea. He was smiling, eyes creased, squinting into the brightness of the light. Skin tanned, hair bleached to the point of whiteness, he looked very like Mike. So like, that from a distance she thought it was him. When she got nearer, she saw that she was mistaken. This man was older, quite a lot older. She realized with a jolt that this was a picture of his uncle, the one who was dead.

He didn't look like most people's idea of an uncle; more like a cousin, or a brother. He stood with his head inclined slightly to one shoulder. He was smiling, as if he and the photographer had just been joking about something. He was leaning forward, hands loosely clasped on the rail in front of him.

It was the hands that caught her attention, or one hand in particular. Finn leaned across the counter, trying to get closer, riveted by the star-shaped marking. Mike's uncle had worn a large tattoo on the back of his right hand. The points extended crossways from the base of his thumb to the blade of his palm; up and down from first knuckle of his ring finger to his wrist. There were other points in between, and each point was marked by an old-fashioned curving letter of the compass.

When she saw it before, she had thought it a web, or star. She had recognized the shape but not the significance. Of course! She could see that now. It was so obvious. . .

"Are you set?" Mike's voice behind her made her jump. "Because we're just about ready. . ."

"What?"

"The boys said you had the money."

"Oh, yes," she fumbled in her pocket. "I – I was just looking at the photo. Is that your uncle?"

"Yes." Mike followed her gaze, taking in the photo, his expression one of admiration mixed up with pride and sorrow.

"The tattoo on his hand. I – I couldn't help but notice. . ."

"The compass? Good isn't it? Must have hurt like hell to have it done. I'd have one, too, if I could get up the guts. Kind of his trademark. What about it?"

"Nothing. It's just . . . unusual." Finn tried to smile. "It caught my attention, that's all."

Mike's uncle was dead. Mike worshipped him. Worshipped his memory. How could she tell him where she had seen that tattoo before?

Chapter Nineteen

When they got back, Maggie Logan wanted a favour from her daughter.

"You know tonight?" She asked, suddenly feeling shy and awkward. "Well, the thing is. . . The thing is. . . Would you babysit for me?"

The question was meant to sound casual, but the last words came out in a rush, leaving Finn puzzled.

"Yes, of course. But. . ."

"Jack's asked me out. Not anything special. Just a pub meal. Nowhere posh, or anything like that. I don't want you getting the wrong idea. . .'

"About what, Mum?" Finn grinned at her mother's confusion. Who was the teenager here? "Go out and have some fun."

Conn and Aidan were less enthusiastic.

"Where's Mum?"

"Upstairs getting ready."

"Getting ready for what?"

"She's going out." Finn replied from the sink where she was finishing off some washing up. "So don't go and pester. If you want something, ask me."

"Going out? Where?"

"With Jack." Both boys looked stunned. "He's taking her out to dinner. Don't look so astonished. I'm going to be babysitting." They both groaned. "Mike's coming up later," Finn added. "He said he'd get a video and pizzas from town."

Conn and Aidan looked at each other, slightly happier.

"How does he know the toppings we like?"

"I'm hungry now."

"I told him what to get." Finn smiled as she dried her hands. "Don't worry. We'll have a nice time. Now go and watch telly and I'll get you a snack or something, and don't bother Mum."

The boys went and Finn turned to the counter, reaching for the bread to make them a sandwich. Once she'd done that, she had better get ready herself. She was cutting and buttering, thinking about nothing, concentrating on what she was doing, when, for no reason, she suddenly stopped and glanced over her shoulder. The boys had gone. There was no one outside, no one in the room with her, but she felt as though someone was watching her, as if she was being overlooked.

Griffiths saw her, clear as if he had been standing outside her window, although he was nowhere near the house. He was not even outdoors. He was in his own house, standing in the big, south-facing room, staring into the glass cabinet. On a wrought-iron stand in front of him stood a hexagonal mirror. It was not made of glass. The surface was dark, as dull as pewter, made of polished stone or sheeted mica.

144

He looked into the surface. At first, his own face looked back, formed from shadows and hollows, like a smoky hologram. He stared on, unblinking and patient. This was no ordinary mirror. Under his dark gaze, the image began to change and change again. First came the girl, red hair snaking down, eyes lowered, brows creased in a little frown of concentration. Then the boy, fair hair dark with water. He had clearly had a shower. He was staring at his own face intently. Obviously looking into a mirror. Griffiths smiled, amused by the idea. As he looked on, the mirror seemed to quiver and darken. The boy's face changed, the bones seemed to shift slightly in their arrangement, brows more prominent, cheek-bones higher, the smooth skin dusted with golden stubble, creases appeared down the side of the mouth and round the pale blue eyes. Griffiths frowned, dropping a velvet cloth over the gaze as the eyes within the mirror began to narrow and the mouth began to smile.

He took up the length of blue rope which lay coiled on the shelf and held it for a moment. The final knot had been reformed, Mike's work acting as a nucleus for something far more elaborate. Griffiths had worked hard on it, wrapping and weaving the rope until the knot resembled a small clenched fist – a *monkey's fist*, the knot was aptly named.

He turned to the window, fingers gripped round the knot as if he was holding a cricket ball. He gazed out, eyes fixed on the point where the two black fangs sprang from the sea, thrusting towards the sky, as if the two were held together in the jaws of some monstrous creature. As he stared out, he began to speak, softly at first, then with rising voice and cadence. The words rang like strange music from his mouth as he recited phrases got by heart, in a language seldom heard, and never written down, but passed from father to son, or grandfather to grandson, always through the male line. In this part of the country, conjurors and cunning men were always male.

As he intoned, the sea wrinkled; across the cliffs the long grass winnowed, and on the trees the leaves moved, swirling into sudden motion as if stirred by an invisible breath. Griffiths smiled his satisfaction and held the last knot even more tightly.

He went back to his special cupboard and took out a small hatchet. The dull-grey steel blade was oiled and spotless. One side was turned in a vicious-looking claw-hook; the other honed to razor keenness. The wooden handle felt warm, snug, the wood worn smooth to the shape of a man's hand, the surface polished by sweat, stained and darkened by sea water and blood. It was the trademark of his ancestors, used by wreckers for centuries, the symbol of the *Gwyr y Bwelli Bach*, the Men of the Little Hatchets. He tested the blade carefully; it could part flesh as easily as putty. Griffiths hefted it up and down, satisfied by its sharpness. It felt good in his hand. It had work to do tonight.

Chapter Twenty

The wind lifted Finn's hair. She swept it back, fitting it behind her ears to stop it whipping about. She and Mike had gone for a walk, leaving the boys munching pizza in front of the video, but the evening was not as warm as it might have been. Midsummer had gone. The air already held a hint of the autumn to come. The sun was setting, staining the sea an odd copper colour, casting a strange yellow light from under a reef of gun-metal cloud.

The tide was on the ebb. In the harbour, the boats jostled and banged against each other in water as dark and dull as old pewter. They moved with an odd jerky, choppy motion which made Finn feel sick just to look at them.

"There's going to be a storm," Mike frowned, staring out to sea. "I told you before."

Finn grinned at his superstition.

Mike shook his head. "It's not just that. It was on the Shipping Forecast before I came out. Gale Warning to Shipping in Finisterre, Sole, Fastnet and Lundy," he recited. "South-westerly Six or Seven, becoming Gale Nine later, strengthening to Storm Force Ten. Moderate becoming poor. The wind is getting up already, and cloud is building out to sea. Just look."

He was right. Even as they stood there, Finn felt the wind getting stronger. You could hear it rustling in the trees, whining in the telephone wires. It was stirring the sand at their feet, picking up litter and bits of paper. Finn turned round. Out on the horizon, banks of cloud were boiling into charcoal thunderheads as fast as on a time-lapse film.

"Perhaps we'd better go back."

"Yeah," Mike agreed, "or there won't be any pizza left."

The boys watched the action movie that Mike had chosen for them, quite oblivious of the storm building outside. Mike was uneasy. He was not happy about the roof. The tiling was only half-finished. He could hear the plastic sheeting flapping and cracking. It was well battened down, but each gust was getting more fierce. The wind would tear at it like fingers, prying underneath the temporary covering, trying to get a purchase, ready to rip it off.

Suddenly, the sound from the TV died. Conn and Aidan let out a howl of protest as the picture dwindled to a tiny dot. They got to their feet, cursing the "crap machine", while Mike stood up and tried the lights, flicking the switch up and down.

Nothing.

"Power cut," he muttered, turning to Finn. "Have you got a torch? Candles? Hurricane lamp?"

She shrugged, palms out in a gesture of helplessness. "I don't know. There could be, but I don't know where."

"I've got a torch." Aidan ran for the door.

"Good lad."

"The battery's out." Aidan came back again, crestfallen. "I just remembered. We used it up in the cave."

"Never mind. I've got one in the pick-up."

He was having to shout. The storm had intensified with great rapidity. The noise of the wind was rising and rising to an insane, blood-chilling, almost human screaming. Rain was hitting the window like bursts of shot. It sounded as if the house was under attack.

Inside the room, no one said anything. They all stared, eyes drawn to the outer darkness. The rain-spattered window seemed to shift in its frame, bulging towards them. For a second it seemed as though it would shatter. Conn and Aidan backed away, edging towards Finn for protection. She put her arms around them, hugging them to her. Then the banshee wailing faded, as if moving on.

"I've got a better idea," Mike said. "Let's get out of here. Take advantage of this lull."

"Where will we go?"

"Up to the pub."

"What about Mum?"

"We'll leave a note for her. Come on, let's go."

Nerys had the candles out, the oil lamps lit and a good fire going. She welcomed them in, settling the boys upstairs with her own.

"It's bad," she said when she came down. "You did the right thing coming up here. Lifeboat's out. Boys have just left. And there's a tanker in trouble off St Mary's."

"That'll be my dad!" Mike looked at her, stricken.

"Don't worry!" Nerys patted his hand. "If anyone can get it in, it'll be him. Nothing you can do. So don't you go distressing yourself."

She offered him a drink, but Mike refused. Nerys shrugged and turned away. No use him fretting. Her family had lived on this coast for centuries. Like her ancestors before her, she was fatalistic about anything to do with the sea. What would be, would be.

Mike sat brooding, staring out at the rain-spattered darkness, rubbing at the back of his hand. Suddenly he got up and began pulling on his waterproofs.

"Where are you going?" Finn asked, puzzled.

He looked down at her, blue eyes bleak and distant. Then he looked round at the others in the room, laughing, joking, talking, drinking.

"I don't know, but I can't stay in here."

Chapter Twenty-one

They struggled across the car park, hanging on to each other, rain driving straight at them.

"I want to get to the headland," Mike said as they got in the pickup. "I have to be there, I have to see. . ."

Good or bad, he had to know what was happening out there in the bay. And it could be bad. If a tanker hit the Vipers. . .

Mike shook his head, unable to find words to describe the consequences of that. A tanker was as big as a football pitch, bigger. If you put it down in the average town it would reach from one end of the main street to the other. It was coming in laden with thousand of tonnes of crude oil. Depending on its position, the turning tide could take it on to the Vipers. In his mind he heard the grinding, rending, tearing of metal as the vicious rocks just below the surface ripped into the hull. Then the sickening smell of oil as it spilled into the ocean, poisoning everything, birds, fish, dolphins, killing the coast for miles around and years to come.

It wasn't just that. It was his dad. He was the pilot. Out there. On that ship. If it hit, he'd get the blame for it. He could lose his job, his licence. His reputation would stand for nothing. . .

The back of his hand itched and throbbed as Mike started the engine. His dad was a proud man, he lived for his job. He stood to lose everything.

"There's a track. Down by the side of Griffiths' house. . ."

Water was sluicing down the lane, covering the tarmac in a slick film of water. Despite his impatience, Mike was forced to drive slowly, keep in low gear, concentrate on his driving.

"Look. Look at that," Finn said as they came round the long bend above Griffiths' house. "There's a light on."

Everywhere else was in darkness but the long low bungalow spilled electrical brightness.

"Maybe he's got a generator."

"It's not that kind of light. Look for yourself."

The light was eerie, strange. It seemed to be moving from one room to another, extending from the windows in misty fingers, shining first blue, then green.

Mike cut the engine, free-wheeled past the row of tall thin conifers, and turned into Griffiths' driveway.

"Where are you going?"

"I want to see what he's up to."

Mike stopped the pick-up and leaned towards the compartment to get his torch. As he reached past her, Finn caught hold of his hand.

"What's this?" Finn whispered.

"Nothing," Mike stared down at the lines he saw there. "Just scratches."

"Are you sure? Let me see."

He placed his hand flat on the wheel, fingers splayed. These were not random scratches, they were taking on a definite shape. There, quite plain, were the cardinal points of the compass, etched over the skin in thin clear lines of purple and red. They seemed to glow in the darkness, taking on light.

"I don't know. . ." Mike flexed his hand. "But I haven't got time to worry about it. Come on, let's go."

He grabbed his torch and eased open the door of the cab. From the house, light glowed intermittently, like shorting electricity.

In the yard, the beam caught the brief pinpoint flare of twinned red eyes. Griffiths' dogs. Mike and Finn flinched back, ready for them to pounce, but the animals made no move towards them; they just whined and cowered further back in their kennels.

They approached the wide-open kitchen door cautiously, Mike first, edging his way in, flicking the torch beam around. The room was a mess. . . The table lay flipped on its side, contents scattered wide; sliced bread fanned like cards, milk pooled across the floor. Mike stepped forward, crunching shards of crockery, playing the flash-light across surfaces tainted and smeared with what looked like sand or mud. There was wetness everywhere, on the table, on the floor, dripping down the walls. The liquid shone black in the torchlight. Mike tested it and tasted salt.

It seemed as though a great flood had surged through. The devastation led them into the hall. The walls were besmirched to shoulder-height and above. Furniture had been knocked over and lay draped with weed from deep in the ocean, long thick straps and thongs of kelp. Sand clumped in lumps on the floor. Footsteps marked the muddy slime, many footsteps, some bare, some boot-printed, trammelling the carpet, turning it to soggy pulp.

The stench was indescribable. Mike and Finn covered their mouths and noses to stop themselves from retching. It smelt like weed heaped on the foreshore. Weed clotted with corrupting matter, decomposing fish, sea birds, the carcasses of sheep and cattle, washed up by the sea and left to rot under a hot sun. The walls on either side were dripping with slime. It was as if some long-dead army, sodden and putrid, had passed this way.

The trail led into the big front room.

Maps and charts had been swept from the mahogany table. They lay, strewn everywhere, a mass of wet paper, torn into tiny pieces. A curling length of rope took their place on the table. Mike recognized it as the blue nylon that he had given Aidan, although the knots *he* had tied had been undone. Only one remained, and that was way beyond his skill. The last knot, large and beautifully crafted, lay in two pieces, bisected by the blade of a little hatchet buried deep in the wood.

Mike turned round to take in the rest of the destruction.

The telescope lay, lens fractured, half inside the glass cabinet it had been used to smash. In the corner there was a heap of what could have once been navigational aids: computer screen, radar, short-wave, satellite. These had come in for special hatred. Crushed into small pieces of twisted metal and plastic, heaped up and kicked about. There was no sign that this was a burglary. Nothing seemed to have been taken; everything seemed to have just been trashed; except for the figurehead that Conn had mentioned. There was no evidence of that.

What had Griffiths been doing in here? Tracking ships by the look of things. But what for? He was a salvage man. Mike looked round again, and his eyes saw more than the modern devices. A dousing pendulum. A knotted cord. A scrying mirror. The tools of the cunning man.

Whatever Griffiths had been doing, there was no sign of him now. Ragged curtains blew out. The window was smashed, the aluminium frame buckled and bent about. Outside lay darkness and the roar of the sea. On the lawn, a myriad glass shards glittered in the torchlight. Whatever came after him, went that way.

"What's happened here?" Finn breathed, hollow-eyed with horror at the scene around her.

"I don't know."

Mike pulled the hatchet from the table, using it to knock the remains of the glass from the window frame. The lines on his hand showed stronger and deeper. They stung and throbbed as though etched by acid.

He climbed into the empty space. "Time to find out."

Chapter Twenty-two

Outside, the grass was flattened, trampled in a wide swathe that lead straight for the edge of the cliff where spray flew in ragged white splashes.

The storm raged with redoubled strength. Mike put his arm round Finn, both of them crouching, bent against a wind that seemed strong enough to whirl them up into the raging darkness like paper dolls. They fought their way as far as they dared towards what seemed like the edge of the world.

The bay in front of them was one seething mass of furious white-water. Huge waves, as tall as houses, pitched and yawed, heaving up in vertical scarps, curling in long overhanging crests, breaking in great plumes of spume which tore off in irregular gobbets and came flying on the wind, spinning to land, lighter than the air that bore it.

"Look," Mike shouted, above the shrill scream of the wind. "Look there!"

He pointed past the line of cliffs backing Yellowstone Cove to the headland jutting out into the sea. *Pentir y Dewin*: the Headland of the Enchanter. A tiny speck of light showed, shining uncertainly, waxing and waning with the unsteady glow of a hand-held lantern.

"There must be someone down there." Finn yelled, but as she stared, the yellow spark wavered and went.

"Further out! Further out!" He had to shout right into her ear.

Out beyond the foaming white water stood a patch of blackness. Waves dashed themselves against it, climbing the sides. It twinkled with lights. It was as if a small island had suddenly appeared out of nowhere. But this was no island. It was a ship. And it was huge.

Griffiths stared out into the darkness at the great bulk of the tanker. He stood with his feet set into slots worn into the top of the ancient cursing stone. The lantern he held had a purely ceremonial function. False lights were not bringing this vessel into shore. His lips moved slightly as he recited the words of power, words strong enough to conjure storms. All around the sea boiled white froth. To his right, Yellowstone Cove was one seething mass. Foam flew up, catching in his hair, flecking his face. Waves dashed against the rocks, reaching right up to his feet, sending spraying spume all over him. Griffiths ignored the chaos around him, his concentration unwavering as he called the ship to him, drawing it on to the Vipers' vicious teeth. For him, as for countless generations of his family, the Vipers was *Afanc*, a living thing, and she was hungry.

He would feed her, as his forefathers had, and he

would be rewarded, just as they had been. After she had taken her fill, the rest would be left for him. In centuries before, it would have been washed up on the shore. Now he would take his reward in the form of salvage. Powerful tugs waited in port, ready for his call. He stood to make a fortune. Financial reward was not the only reason that he'd brought this train of events into being. His other reason was more personal. It was called Treherne.

Out beyond the wide curving bay, Mike's father stood on the bridge of the giant tanker. The instruments had all gone haywire: the gyro compass spun useless, the instrument panels showed a mass of jumbled figures, radar screens and sonar blurred in meaningless patterns. It was as if some tremendous force was jamming everything, as if 147,000 tonnes of ship was being dragged to shore by some giant magnet. Only his pilot's sense was left to guide it, to keep it off the jagged reef of the Vipers, the rocks would rip the bottom right out of it. Wind and tide would break the vessel, rendering the steel hull as fragile as an egg shell.

His first concern would be the safety of the crew. After that. . .

The consequences were almost too terrible to think about. Tens of thousands of tonnes of crude oil pouring into the sea, leaking out of the stricken vessel to form a huge slick, spreading inexorably, poisoning the seas, polluting the coastline.

He had no thought of his own safety, or his job, or reputation, as he contemplated this destruction. His duty was to captain, crew and vessel. His mind ran on to contingency plans for rescue and damage limitation. It was too late for anything else. Too late to stop the disaster from happening.

He stood, stilled in concentration, waiting for the first shuddering vibration, the sound of liquid being forced under pressure, the rending grind of rock on metal, the unmistakable smell of oil. . .

Griffiths smiled his satisfaction. Impact could not be more than seconds away. He redoubled his concentration. Everything he had would go into this one last effort. He became so completely absorbed by his task that he failed to register another presence. Something nearer. Near enough to touch him on the shoulder. Something. Or someone.

Griffiths turned his head and stared, transfixed, lips suddenly stiff, words reduced to mumbled gibberish. A hand grasped his shoulder, the skin white and livid, etched with a tattoo, red and blue. The cardinal points of the compass showed in curling black capitals stretched tight over sharply ridged bone and tendon. He tried to turn away, dreading to see who the hand belonged to, but the strong fingers gripped like steel claws, biting into his flesh, forcing him round. His own features contorted in recognition. This creature had stalked his dreams, coming back to the Salt House night after night, making it so Griffiths rarely ever slept, forcing him to build the New House. He had not visited there; Griffiths had thought that he was safe from him. Until tonight.

"Hello, Griff. Remember me?"

No flesh remained on the face. Teeth gleamed like pearls in bones ribbed and white as shell. Griffiths went to speak, but his own voice refused to function. The hand tightened, snapping bone and piercing flesh. Something glinted deep in the eyeless sockets, a gleaming amber red.

Griffiths lips pulled back in a scream that never left his throat. A crowd was massing about him. A numberless, ghastly crew of mariners, fishermen and sailors; all lost at sea, or drowned in the bay, or hacked on the shore, their lives cut short by Griffiths and his clan of wreckers. They had come for him. With the storm he had summoned them and they had come searching, moving up past the Salt House, sweeping through his new house, then out and along the cliff. They had found him here, at the Headland of the Enchanter, standing on the cursing stone of his forefathers, and here they would take him.

The spectral figures came out of the darkness, their figures outlined in glimmering phosphorescence. Their sea-rotted clothes were ragged and torn, showing the bleached bones and bloated flesh of the long dead. Their skeletal fingers gripped great curved hooks and razor-sharp hatchets. The lantern fell from his nerveless hand and Griffiths threw up his arms, trying to defend himself, but his efforts were futile.

He sank to his knees, then to the floor, overwhelmed by the blows of those wrecked on this treacherous shore.

A huge wave rose up, swamping the headland. It broke in a furious spray of spume over the jutting point of land and when they looked again, the speck of light was there no more.

"Look." Mike gripped Finn's shoulder and turned her away from where the huge tanker hovered on the edge of the Vipers. "Look out there," he whispered, his voice trembling, hushed with awe.

Out in the bay, the meaningless random white-water patterns on the sea's surface seemed to be joining, coalescing, taking on the shape and outline of a spectral ship. It came swiftly, heeled over slightly, scribbled on the sea's surface as if made from the very waves it rode. The hull was as midnight-black as the precipitous slopes of water, the sails and rigging as white and delicate as spindrift spray, as it ran in from the open sea, heading into the maelstrom of Yellowstone Cove.

The storm seemed to die as the ghostly spectre neared the shore. The clouds tore and parted. Light from a bone-white sliver of moon leant the scene an eerie, beautiful grandeur. The seas were still mountainous, but the great sailing ship rode them easily, right to the towering cliffs. There it waited at anchor, as if safe in harbour, holding its position as dark figures leaped from the land and swarmed down the rigging on to the deck. Then the spectral craft heeled and sailed under the cliff. They could plainly see the figurehead, a woman's painted face and breasts thrust out under the bowsprit. The nameplate on her side proclaimed her to be *Anna Marie.* She turned against the wind and sailed right out of the cove as swiftly as she had come.

As Finn and Mike watched from the shore, clouds returned to obscure the moon. Out in the bay, the spectral vessel began to disappear, merging into the endless chaotic movement of the sea.

Chapter Twenty-three

"What was that?"

Finn turned to Mike, her face pinched and white under the jutting peak of her hood. She was drenched to the skin, long strands of escaping hair whipped round her face, hanging down in tangled rats' tails. She was shivering. Mike put his arms round her, drawing her close. His warmth was comforting.

"I don't know." He shook his head. "I really don't."

Over his shoulder, Finn glanced up at the house. The big window looked like it had been punched out by a giant hand.

"What happened to Griffiths?"

"I haven't got a clue. But, right now, I'm more worried about you. Come on," he held her tighter, "let's get back to the track."

"What do you think was after him?" Finn looked up into his face.

"God knows."

Mike's eyes became distant, clouded. He gazed out at the sea beyond her. He had the distinct feeling that, whatever it was, it had gone now. He preferred not to think about what had happened to Griffiths, but felt pretty sure that he would not be coming back from it. Somewhere distant, a dog howled. It could be one of Griffiths' mutts. The sound was plaintive, full of loss. Sometimes dogs know things that humans don't.

Mike kept his arm round Finn, helping her down the slippery cliff path. The wind had died almost to nothing. The rain had stopped. The only moisture was dripping from the tall pines towering stark against a clearing sky, motionless and paralyzed. One of the branches creaked and, on the beach, the surf boomed loud in the sudden quietness.

A bend in the path brought them to a point above the harbour. Mike stopped to take in the destruction the storm had brought to the boats moored there. They had been tossed and thrown about like toys in a paddling pool. Some of the smaller ones, including the *Little Jenny*, had been thrown right out of the water; they lay stranded, strewn about like so many shells. His eyes searched the chaos, looking for Griffiths' boat with its distinctive white hull, long-prowed, sleek and narrow.

"What are you looking at?"

"The harbour."

"Oh, Mike," Finn spotted the *Little Jenny*, "I'm sorry. . ."

"It doesn't look too bad. Anyway, that's not what I was looking at. I was looking for Griffiths' boat. I don't see it. Wait a minute. . ." His gaze shifted away from the harbour, out into the bay. "There's something out there."

His sharp eyes had seen a shape in the water. A boat. It was coming in broadside, drifting, helpless, thrown from one wave to another. It was hard to tell what kind of craft it was. The mast had gone, the superstructure sheered off. But it was still afloat, sometimes visible, sometimes hidden, bobbing up and then disappearing in the troughs between the huge lines of rollers sweeping to shore.

"There could be survivors."

Mike scanned the sea around the stricken vessel, looking for the flash of a beacon, a splash of bright colour, the yellow or orange of life-raft or jacket. When he could find nothing, his gaze shifted again, this time to the beach. He narrowed his eyes, squinting, wishing he had night sights, binoculars, anything to help his search. He was looking for something human in size and shape, but the dark blobs he could see could be rocks, timber, piles of weed, or any other thing the storm had tossed up on to the beach.

Then he saw something. Its starfish sprawl suggested it could be human.

"There's at least one person." He craned forward, trying to see better. "There maybe others. . ."

"What about emergency services? The lifeboat. . ."

Mike waved his arm impatiently, taking in a world empty of other human presence.

"Do you see them?"

"We could go to the house. We could call. . ."

"The phone lines are down." He shook his head. "We have to go ourselves. We have to help, render any assistance we can. We have to, Finn. Come on!"

Mike was already running for the beach, answering an unspoken call, following the age-old code of those who lived by the sea.

Finn took one look towards the Salt House, standing dark and empty, and then followed him down to the beach.

She hesitated on the edge of the slick, shiny length of sand. It was like every nightmare that she'd ever had. The air, salt thick and water-laden, caught in her throat. All around her, the thunder of breaking surf was huge and constant, beating in her ears, pounding in her brain, echoing the thud and surge of her own blood. She ought to go after Mike, run to catch him, offer help but, when it came down to it, she did not know if she could. . .

Mike felt no such hesitation as he ran along the hard sand. He doubled his speed, stretching his long legs, sprinting at full capacity, as he saw that he'd been right, it *was* a body sprawled out there on the shore.

It looked like a man. He was lying face down, Dark hair, matted with sand, snaked down from his head like clinging clumps of weed. Mike stopped for a second to catch his breath and then bent over, grasping the inert form by the shoulder, ready to turn him, to see if he was alive. . .

Mike pulled, but the man was heavy. He was big,

tall. His clothes were saturated, sodden with water, his lifeless body a dead weight. He heaved, this time managing to lift the shoulders and chest partly off the sand, the face coming away with a slight sucking sound. Mike didn't give much for his chances. The back of the head looked suspiciously pulpy and a closer examination showed that his outer garments were shredded, exposing deep wounds and bloody lacerations. This man had been bashed and buffeted, badly cut up on the rocks. Still, one more lift would do it. Mike redoubled his grip and heaved again. People survived in all kinds of conditions and it was his duty to check for signs of life.

His last effort managed to turn the body. It flopped on to its back like a flaccid crab. The guy did not seem to be breathing. Mike was pretty sure that he was dead, but he swallowed hard and went down on one knee, putting a hand to the neck, averting his gaze from a face ripped and mutilated beyond recognition. Beneath a clinging crust of sand, the mouth hung broken-jawed and slack. The eyes were half-closed, white bulged below the lids, showing in hard-boiled egg crescents. Wounds gaped like tattered mouths in the grey sodden flesh. There was no pulse. The flesh was cold to the touch, clammy as a chicken carcass. Mike knelt for a moment, suddenly nauseous, his breath coming out in long shudders.

He moved to stand up, but his legs were shaking. He stopped at a half crouch and put out a hand to steady himself. As he did so, he glanced down at the body.

The eyes were now open; liquid pools of glittering darkness were staring back at him. What was left of the man's face parted in a lopsided grin. Mike let out a cry of horrified recognition. He was looking into the ruined features of Mr Griffiths.

Mike sprang to his feet, but a hand shot out and grabbed him by the wrist. Mike let out a cry and pulled back, but he found himself clamped by unbelievable strength. The creature was up on all fours now, dragging at him. Mike found it hard to keep his stance. He was being wrenched forward, his feet slipping and sliding in the wet sand. The thing was moving crabwise, low to the ground, dragging him to the place where mountainous surf pounded the shore. Mike struggled, fighting for his life, but the harder he fought the tighter the circling fingers gripped his wrist, digging in, biting deep into the flesh like steel cuffs.

"Help!" Mike screamed, yelling as loud as he could. "Somebody help me!"

His voice was drowned, swallowed by the hollow boom and roar of the surf on the shore. Storm-whipped waves reared up, as high as houses, before crashing down in an explosion of spray. Once he was caught in there, dragged by the crushing, grinding undertow, he would stand no chance. He stared in abhorrence at Griffiths' shredded features; he would end up looking like that.

Mike's horror, his frantic struggling, seemed to amuse Griffiths. Flaps of flesh lifted, teeth showing to the jaw-bone as his grin widened. A sound came from his throat, somewhere between a gurgle and a chuckle. Words came through in a kind of liquid bubbling.

"No one can help you now."

Chapter Twenty-four

Finn fought with herself, trying to overcome her fear. Mike was crouched over a shape lying prone on the sand. He had found something, or someone. It could be a dead body, Finn shuddered, but what if it was alive? He was pulling at it now, struggling. She couldn't just stand here dithering, leaving him to cope alone. What if it was too heavy for him? She stepped on to the squelching, sucking sand. There was no one else. She had to go.

Finn had long legs and was a fast runner. The sand, saturated and scrubbed, ribbed and hard beneath her feet, provided a good surface. She ran swiftly, not looking up until she was nearing the place where Mike had stopped.

When she raised her head, what she saw made her falter. She could see by the shape and outline that Mike had found a body. The two figures were half-merged together. It looked, at first, as though Mike was trying to pull it up, but something didn't seem right. There was a backwards, forwards, tug-of-war motion, as though the pulling was not all one way, as if the other person was pulling on him, dragging. . .

Then she heard him scream.

Finn set off again, running even faster, ignoring a stitch starting and the breath labouring in her chest. The struggle was getting more one-sided, Mike was losing his footing, sliding towards the line of surf pounding the shore.

"Help! Somebody help me!" The cry came thin and frail above the sea's deep throated roar.

Mike was lying full out now, being dragged by some huge crab-like creature. It was not until Finn got nearer that she could see that it had once been human. She looked away from the ghastly grinning face, searching frantically for some kind of weapon, a piece of driftwood, anything to beat the creature off. There was nothing. The beach was scoured clean.

Then she saw it, a bright object lying between small rivulets of running water, the surface shining silver in the thin moonlight. The little hatchet. It must have fallen out of Mike's coat pocket.

Finn snatched it up and ran towards the struggling figures. Mike was losing the contest. He was being dragged like a small child, weak and helpless, towards the terrifying thunder of the surf. Finn was his only hope. She tried to hold the hatchet firm as she advanced on the creature, but her whole body was shaking. Her arm seemed to go into spasm, the axe jerking and waving about in her hand.

The creature had Mike gripped at the wrist. She forced herself to look at it. Look at its face. It was only then she realized: this *thing* was Griffiths. Or had been.

For it was not alive any more. No human being could survive such hideous wounds and still retain such enormous strength. In that second, she knew. When it had finished with Mike, it would be back for her, too.

She stood mesmerized, unable to move. Her fingers relaxed and the axe was about to fall from her nerveless hand, when some other force seemed to take her over. Her consciousness seemed to flee from the horror confronting her to be replaced by another. She tightened her grip on the hatchet. It felt snug in her hand. Right. Like an extension of her own arm. She stepped forward, measuring the distance carefully, mentally marking where to strike. Her eyes focused on a spot on the forearm just above the wrist. She would only be able to strike once. The blade was wickedly sharp. Her aim must be true, or she risked severing Mike's hand instead.

She raised the axe and brought it down swiftly with a short chopping motion. The blow jarred up her arm into her shoulder. There was a sickening thunk as the blade connected with bone. One glance told her that the limb had not been cleanly severed, it was hanging on by skin and muscle. Finn brought the blade down again. The thing that had been Griffiths gave a gurgling scream. He staggered backwards towards the rising surf, blood spraying from the severed limb.

For one horrifying second the grip of his hand on Mike did not slacken. Then the fingers went flaccid, releasing their grasp, and the hand fell, leaking blood into the sand. Finn grabbed Mike, dragging him upright, as the water rose to a solid wall. He staggered against her and they stumbled back up the beach. Behind them the wave reached its full height and fell, crashing in a rolling tumble of white water. Pebbles clacked as the wave dragged back. When they turned to stare at the receding water, there was no sign of Griffiths. All that remained was his blood, streaking the foaming water, staining the tide with red.

Chapter Twenty-five

Finn dropped the hatchet and put her arms round Mike. He could not stop shaking. She held him, whispering that it was all over, it would be all right now.

Neither of them spoke after that. They just clung to each other, each glad to be alive, to have survived. Finn could not quite believe how precious Mike suddenly seemed to her.

The words had not been minted that could express what Mike was feeling. He had never felt like this before. He was filled with admiration for Finn's bravery, her coolness, for what she had done. He owed his life to her. Tears fringed his lashes as he held her tighter. He was shaking, trembling all over. Shock and first love have similar effects.

The storm had died to nothing. There was no wind, no sound except for the boom of the sea. They went back to the Salt House and found it much as they had left it, dark and deserted, plastic sheeting hanging from the roof in tatters. There was a battery-operated lamp on the kitchen table. Mike recognized it as Jack's, kept in the boot of his car for emergencies. Finn's note had disappeared. Her mum must have come back and, finding no one home, gone up to the pub.

"You're soaking," Mike said, as he lit the lamp. "You need to get dry. Change your clothes."

"How's your hand?"

"It doesn't hurt any more, but. . ."

He held it out for her to see, fingers spread. The star-shaped mark was fading, but it still showed faintly. It would never go completely. It would remain as a pale tracing, to remind him of this night and the things that had happened.

"You poor thing." Finn took his hand and touched it to her lips.

"Come on," he said gruffly. "You'll catch your death standing around like this. Time to get some dry things on."

"What are you going to do?"

"I'll put my clothes in the tumble dryer."

"No electricity."

"Oh, yes." He laughed, stroking her hair away from her face. "I forgot."

He put his arms round her again and kissed her. His face was cold, but his lips were warm and tasted of salt.

"You can wear some of mine." Finn murmured. "Come upstairs, let's see what we can find."

The *Smuggler's Rest* was buzzing, candles on every table. Half the village was in there, creating quite a party atmosphere.

"Where have you two been?" Maggie Logan asked when Finn and Mike came in.

"Up at the Point," Mike explained. "Trying to see the tanker. My dad's on it." He turned to his uncle. "Any news?"

Jack shook his head. "I'm going down to the Port Authority, see what's doing. Want to come?"

"Yes." Mike held Finn's hand for a moment or two longer, then let go. "I'll see you later."

Maggie watched, eyebrows raised, catching the look exchanged between Mike and her daughter. When did this happen? All of a sudden their relationship seemed to have warped from border-line dislike to undying passion. She smiled. Sometimes things just went that way when you were young.

"What are you smiling about?"

"Nothing." Maggie turned to her daughter. "Are you all right?"

"Yes, sure. Why do you ask?"

"I don't know. You just look – different." Her mother toyed with her glass. "If you don't mind me asking. . . Why is he wearing your clothes?"

"Oh," Finn was ready for that. "We went down to the harbour. Mike wanted to see what had happened to the *Little Jenny*. We got soaked getting down there, so we went back to the house. Mike didn't have any spare clothes, so I lent him some of mine. Trousers are a bit short, of course. . ."

"I see."

"What about you?" Finn looked back at her mother. "How did your date go? Did you have a nice time?"

"Great. Except the storm kind of spoilt it. When we got back and found the house deserted, I nearly panicked," Maggie smiled ruefully. "Well, did panic, actually. Good thing Jack was with me."

"I knew you'd be worried, but I couldn't see what else to do. All the power went and I thought the storm was going to tear the house apart. Mike suggested coming up here might be safer, because of the state of the roof."

"That's what we thought. It was a good move."

"Boys OK?"

"Fine. Settled in with Nerys' two. Getting on like a house on fire when we got here. They are more or less the same age."

"That's nice."

"Isn't it? Aidan doesn't make friends easily and Conn can get, well, a bit argumentative. It would be so nice if they could make friends here."

"Steady on," Finn laughed. "They've only been together for one night. Plenty of time yet for them to fall out. Why is it so important? It's not as if we're stay-ing here. . ." Finn glanced up, trying to read her mother's face in the flickering candlelight. "Are we?"

"I thought we might." Maggie pushed her hair back, her eyes alight with excitement. "There's nothing to keep us back home. You're going to sixth-form college, Conn's in his last year of juniors, Aidan hates his school anyway. I never wanted to *stay* in that house, not after your dad left. It was only while I got myself sorted, and I feel sorted now."

"Since when? This is very sudden."

"Not really. I've been going over it in my mind, thinking about it for some time."

"You never said."

Her mother shrugged, "I hadn't really decided."

"And you have now?"

"I think so. What do you feel about it? Staying here, I mean. Would you mind? Of course, if you did, I wouldn't consider it. . ."

"It's OK, Mum." Finn put her hand out to her. "I think it's a good idea."

"What about the boys?"

"They'll go for it, I'm sure."

"Oh, I'm so glad you think that, Finn." Her mother's face broke into a radiant smile. "With any luck I'll be able to get a job teaching and Nerys and Jack say the schools are very good, so you and the boys will be all right. I feel so energized here, Finn." She reached for her daughter's hand. "You have no idea. I might even start my own work again. I haven't felt this way in years."

"Where will we live?"

"The Salt House, of course. Carole will let me have it for a small rent, she might even sell it to me eventually. Meanwhile, until the repairs are finished, we'll be staying here. . ."

"OK." Finn stood up. "Just as long as I know. Which room am I in? I think I'll go up, I'm really tired."

"Second on the right, first floor. Nerys will show you, And, Finn?"

"Yes," Finn turned to face her mother.

"You could have done a lot worse. I think Mike's lovely. He's a really nice boy."

Chapter Twenty-six

In the morning, Nerys brought copies of the papers over from the Post Office.

Eco Disaster Narrowly Averted

Last night, the supertanker, *Sea Monarch*, carrying 130,000 tonnes of crude oil from the Forties Field to the port of Danford Haven, was metres away from causing a major ecological disaster in one of the country's most sensitive conservation areas. Environmental agencies were alerted as the ship fought storm-force winds and heavy sea conditions to avoid running aground on the Vipers, a notorious reef and hazard to shipping off Druid's Head.

Unconfirmed reports suggest that the Liberian-registered vessel, crewed by Russians, had developed a steering problem and this had been compounded by other system failures. A spokesman for the local Port Authority said that it was too early to comment, but it seemed that lack of power and steering capacity, combined with faulty radar and atrocious weather conditions had contributed to a situation "unique in my experience". He paid tribute to the Pilot, Mr David Treherne, whose "prompt action saved the day."

Mr Treherne himself asserts that he was "only doing my job".

This stretch of water has experienced several recent disasters, or near disasters. Nearby marine environments contain many rare species, including one of Britain's largest colonies of harbour porpoises. The adjacent coastline is home to half a million seabirds as well as colonies of grey seals. The near grounding of the *Sea Monarch* is bound to add to the growing number of calls for new safety regulations to govern the movement of potentially hazardous cargoes in environmentally sensitive areas.

"Hi, how are you feeling?" Mike came in as Finn was finishing her breakfast reading the paper.

"OK, I guess."

"Did you sleep?"

"Yes," Finn looked thoughtful, as though considering. "Yes. Yes, I did. I'm glad your dad's all right," she added, nodding towards the newspaper spread open on the table.

Mike grinned. "So am I. It was a close call, by all accounts."

"I've been thinking. About last night—"

"What?" Perhaps she'd changed her mind. Perhaps she didn't feel like he did. Mike lost his smile.

"Not that." Finn took his hand. "About Griffiths. Did you say anything?"

Mike shook his head, and gave a warning glance towards the kitchen door. Nerys had ears like super-sensitive listening devices. She didn't miss much.

"Funny you should be talking about him," she said as she bustled in. "Jim's just come back with his post. Says his place is deserted. Doors open. Dogs howling. It's criminal the way he keeps 'em cooped up in kennels, big dogs like that. The place is a terrible tip, Jim says, mess everywhere. Goodness knows what's been going on. He's called the police. Can I get you anything else?"

Finn shook her head, pushing away her plate.

"You ought to eat up. You're too skinny. Mike?"

"I've already eaten, thanks."

A moment ago he'd been starving, but a sudden vision of Griffiths, the way they had seen him last night, took away his appetite.

Griffiths' body was never found. The only evidence to account for his disappearance was the absence of his boat from the harbour and a few bits of wreckage washed up in the bay which were identified as coming from his cruiser. He must have taken his boat out, so the official explanation went, thinking perhaps to move it to a safer mooring, but he had got caught in the storm and been unable to get out of the bay.

But why he would do such a foolish thing in such dangerous sea conditions, with storm-force winds threatening, nobody could answer. As to the damage to his house? That was even harder to explain. Burglary was suggested, but there was no evidence to back it. Nothing seemed to be missing. It looked like vandalism, but apart from a few smudges, no finger-prints were found that belong to anyone other than Griffiths. The damage must have been self-inflicted. But who would do such a thing? The same man who took a boat out in a Storm Force Ten, the locals said, and the police were inclined to agree. What other explanation could there be?

It was enough to satisfy the Coroner's Office. Finn and Mike agreed between them: they would never tell anyone what they saw that night. If any in the village had an opinion which differed from the official expla-nation, they kept quiet about it. The sea had claimed another one, that's how most people saw it. Eventually a marker would appear in the churchyard, paid for out of Griffiths' estate. Plain granite, with just his name and the date of his disappearance, set on the north side next to the rest of his clan.

Maggie, Finn, Conn and Aidan stayed at the *Smugglers'* until the Salt House was ready for them. Finn was dreading going back, terrified in fact, but she need not have worried. As soon as she walked in, she knew that the house was different. It was not just the new roof, or the smell of paint and wood, it was the atmosphere. It was lighter, fresher, as though the place had been cleansed. Her nights were no longer disturbed. The ghosts had gone from the shore; they would not come back any more. Her dreams were peaceful.

Jack spent a lot of time there now. He and Mum were supposed to be converting the outhouses into a studio. He came down after work to help her and that spilled into staying for dinner and sharing a bottle of wine. A labour of love you could call it, and the way he looked at her, you wouldn't be far from the mark.

Finn didn't mind. In fact, she was glad. He was a nice bloke, and Mum deserved a life. The boys were quite happy about it. They really liked Jack. All they could talk about was fishing, sailing and surfing, and he owned the shop.

They were with Bryn and Huw, Nerys's sons, most of the time – which left Finn free to spend the rest of her summer with Mike.

Come Autumn, Conn had started at the village school, Aidan at the comprehensive in town. They settled in quickly, and seemed quite happy. Mum got a part-time job at the local art college, with the promise of full-time after Christmas. She was still seeing Jack. Their relationship had lost its novelty value. They were quite a fixture now.

And Finn? She went to the local sixth-form college. It was OK. The courses were what she wanted, and the other students were all right. She'd made friends with a couple of them and was even enjoying something resembling a social life.

Every week she got postcards. She was building up quite a collection, a collage on the bedroom wall. They came from all over, telling her how the surf was in Mexico, California, Hawaii and New Zealand. He still had half the globe to go yet, but when he came back, she'd be waiting for him.

Acknowledgements

Thanks to Cristine and Julia for help of a Welsh kind, and to Penny and Phil in Devon, and to John Bowers for lending me his book.